Love's Compass
Book Two
Finding Hope

Melanie D. Snitker

For God has not given
us a spirit of fear,
but of power, and of
love, and of a sound mind.
2 Timothy 1:7

- MDS

This is a work of fiction. Names, places, characters, and events in this novel are a result of the author's imagination. Any similarities to actual events and persons, living or dead, are purely coincidental. Any trademarks, product names, service marks, or named features are the property of their respective owners and are only used for reference.

http://www.melaniedsnitker.com/

ISBN: 1514309033
ISBN-13: 978-1514309032

For all of my readers who
have been touched by cancer.
Your strength, courage, and determination
is what makes you a true hero.

Contents

Contents

Acknowledgments

Special thanks to the wonderful individuals who helped to make this book possible: Doug Snitker, Sandy Crump, Steph Dowlen, Denny Deady, and Ashlee Enz. Your input was invaluable and I'm incredibly thankful for each of you!

Chapter One

Lexi Chandler replaced the lid on the can of coffee grounds. Her finger touched the switch that flipped the coffee maker on again. She watched long enough to see a layer of the dark fluid start to flow, covering the bottom of the glass pot.

Juan Ramirez, a resident on duty at the Kitner Memorial Hospital emergency room, breezed into the break room.

His shoulders sagged with relief as he grabbed a cup and leaned against the counter, all before the door swung closed again.

"As soon as I heard you'd come on shift, I finished stitching up Miss Wilkham's hand and headed in here." He said it all without averting his eyes from the liquid gold. He reminded Lexi of a vulture sitting on a tree, hunched over as he waited for his prey to wander into view.

She held back a smile and mustered a serious

voice. "You're just in time. I found a different brand of coffee to try. Hazelnut something."

Ramirez's gaze snapped to her face and he nearly dropped his cup in the process. If looks could kill, there would be a chalk outline of her body on the floor right now.

"I'm joking, Ramirez."

He forced a smile that didn't quite reach his eyes and turned back to the pot. She could have sworn he was analyzing it for clues about the contents. If she hadn't been standing right there, he probably would have stuck his nose over the top for a whiff. "Don't kid about the coffee, Chandler."

Before it had filled halfway, Ramirez gave up waiting. He pulled the pot out and placed his cup underneath the stream, drops of brown splashing onto the white appliance.

The break room door opened again and Finnegan, one of the attending physicians, walked in. He wasted no time in pouring a cup of coffee from the pot waiting to be placed back on the stand.

"It's good to have you back, Chandler."

"It's nice to know everyone appreciates me for my nursing skills." Lexi's words were laced with sarcasm. Truthfully, she didn't mind that her coworkers preferred it when she made the coffee. In a world of twelve hour shifts and insanely busy days, her ability to make the best cup of coffee in the hospital gave her a degree of influence. It was difficult to not take advantage of that kind of control at times — especially when it meant giving Ramirez a panic attack over an imaginary change in coffee beans.

Finnegan took a swig from his mug and pointed a finger at her. "I have tickets for the game on Saturday if you'd like to go."

Lexi suppressed a sigh. If she got a dollar for every time the man asked her out on a date, she could afford a steak dinner. "I'm not interested, Finnegan."

"Can't blame a guy for trying." He winked at her on his way back out.

And trying and trying. Lexi rolled her eyes. He had perseverance, she'd give him that. He'd been asking her to go out with him for months, along with every other woman in the hospital sporting a pulse. He flashed that smile full of white teeth and women seemed to melt into a puddle. Not her. She preferred a man with a personality. A little class never hurt, either.

When Doctor Ramirez felt his cup was full enough, he replaced the pitcher and took a gulp. He winced when the hot liquid hit his throat, held the cup out to her with a nod, and took his leave.

Another satisfied customer.

Her prowess as a coffee barista was discovered entirely by chance. The nurse who usually started the coffee quit. In an attempt to help her coworkers, Lexi started out by following the directions on the back of the can. She listened to other nurses and doctors, heard their opinions about the flavor, and adjusted. Before she knew it, people were lining up for the stuff when she was on shift.

Lexi didn't drink it herself. In her opinion, there was no amount of sugar that could make the brew palatable.

A smile on her face, Lexi stepped into the hallway. Kate, one of her fellow registered nurses, was shaking her head. "You make the rest of us look bad."

Lexi shrugged. "It's not my fault I'm the only one

in this place that can make a decent cup of coffee. It's a gift."

"Mmm hmm. Speaking of gifts, we're having a baby shower for Celeste during her shift a week from today. I saw you were scheduled to work then, too. Think you can make it?"

Lexi tried to picture the calendar in her mind. "I should be able to. What's the plan?"

Kate held up a hand. "I'm handling the cake and decorations. All the nurses are pitching in to buy her the stroller set she wants on her registry. Wren is collecting the money. We're aiming for twenty-five dollars per person if you can swing it."

The subject of their conversation appeared at the end of the hall. Celeste's brightly-colored scrubs covered in butterflies were hard to miss. Especially when they covered a protruding belly.

"We have a six-year-old boy in room four. He's experiencing respiratory distress — they just arrived."

Lexi nodded. "Thanks, Celeste. I've got it." She put a hand on Kate's shoulder. "That should be doable. I'll get my share to Wren tomorrow."

Kate gave her a nod and Lexi jogged down the hall.

Lexi was good with kids. She had a knack for helping them feel at ease in a situation that was anything but pleasant. It was because of that skill she was often requested to help evaluate pediatric patients brought in to the ER.

The moment she entered the exam room, she picked up the chart and glanced at it. The boy – Cade — wore a shirt with Darth Vader on it. She observed him a moment as a woman she assumed to be his mother kept an arm around his shoulder.

He was propped up on the hospital bed and each breath he took was a struggle. His nose flared and his stomach caved in on inhalation. He was having an asthma attack and they needed to get it under control.

"Hey, Cade. I'm Nurse Lexi. Are you having a tough time breathing today?"

The boy nodded, his eyes wide. His lips were not as pink as they should have been.

The woman lovingly ruffled Cade's hair, her eyes relaying the worry she felt while she kept her voice calm and collected. "When the rescue inhaler didn't work, I brought him right in."

"Moms always know best. It's a good thing you did, Mrs. Lewis."

Lexi put an oxygen monitor on Cade's pointer finger. A glance at the numbers confirmed her suspicion. "Well, Mrs. Lewis, oxygen levels are lower than we like to see. Is Cade allergic to anything?"

"Dogs. But he hasn't been around any lately that I know of."

Lexi jotted down a few notes. "We're going to get him started on a breathing treatment right away. We'll get this under control in no time." She picked up the oxygen mask and turned to her young patient. "Meanwhile, I want you to put this on until I get back." His eyes widened and he shook his head. "Trust me, Cade. It's like the mask Darth Vader wears." She made exaggerated breathing sounds and mustered her deepest voice. "'Luke, I am your father.'"

Cade rewarded her with a weak smile and she placed the mask over his mouth and nose.

She turned to his mother. "I'll be right back with that breathing treatment."

"Thank you."

~

Lance Davenport leaned his chair back on two legs. He surveyed the hospital cafeteria, keeping his eyes on the double doors.

He wasn't sure of Lexi's schedule, but he knew she was working today. Since the cafeteria always served Mexican food on Wednesdays, she'd show up for lunch sooner or later. The woman loved her tacos.

Another five minutes passed before she appeared. She strode into the room, her purple scrubs matching several others in the room. She pushed some of her short hair behind a delicate ear. Her hair was nearly black — it'd been like that since they were kids. Dark as molasses.

Lexi picked up a tray and advanced towards the taco bar. By the time she'd gotten to the register, he was waiting, holding a twenty out to the cashier.

Lexi's brown eyes swung to his. "Lance, you're about the last person I expected to see here." She nodded towards his hand holding the change. "Thank you."

Lance followed her to a table and took the chair opposite her. "Not a problem."

"What's up?"

He watched her take a bite of refried beans. "Can't a friend come by and say hello?"

She raised an eyebrow at him.

He chuckled. They may have known each other since he was in the third grade, but it was Tuck, her younger brother, who'd been Lance's best friend. In fact, Tuck was like a brother to him. That alone had saved Lance's sanity more times than he could count while living in a household with four sisters.

Lexi was two years older than Lance. As kids, he'd admired her. She had a heart for helping others and exuded confidence in everything she did. Throw in her ready smile, long arms, and the graceful way she moved, it was no wonder every boy in school had had a crush on her.

Lance had been no exception.

The woman had only gotten prettier over the years. Long, dark lashes framed eyes that had a knack for recognizing the needs of people around her. But it was her smile that had the power to light up a room.

"Okay, you got me. I came with a reason. Do I need to bring anything to Tuck and Laurie's welcome home party?"

His best friend had gotten married the weekend before. The new couple were away on their honeymoon. A week at a ranch in the mountains. It was not a typical honeymoon destination, but it fit both of them well.

The Chandler family had a welcome home party planned for them Sunday evening and Lance was invited. He attended a lot of the family gatherings. Normally, he didn't think twice about them. He was out of his element on this one, though. This was his first friend to have gotten married, and he wasn't sure what to expect.

"Don't worry. It'll be a simple pizza party. No gifts or anything special. Bring sodas if you want to."

"I can do that." He thought about how Lexi always chose tea over carbonated drinks. "I'll bring a jug of iced tea, too."

Her dark brown eyes sparkled as she smiled. "I

appreciate that. Did you already eat?"

Lance's eyes followed hers to the empty table space in front of him. "Yeah, earlier. I didn't want to miss you."

Her fork stalled on its way to her mouth. "How long were you waiting?"

"It doesn't matter. I'll be there right at five. Can't wait to see them. It feels like forever."

"It sure does. I imagine even more so for you after the last couple of months. How's your father doing?"

Lance's thoughts drifted to Peter Davenport. A strong man who had done carpentry work all of his life, Peter had spent many hours showing Lance how to build things. After three generations, there were a lot of memories attached to his dad's workshop.

While Peter always supported Lance's decision to be a police officer, there had been some disappointment when he didn't take over the family business.

And then, in moments, everything changed. His mom, Vera, had called. His dad had had a stroke.

He survived, but the weakness on one side of his body had rendered him unable to work.

Lance's world changed that day, too. He wasn't about to let the family business fade to a memory.

A week after his father's stroke, Lance gave his resignation at the police department. Two weeks later, he became the new owner of Davenport Carpentry.

"Dad's okay. Therapy is helping him a lot. He's frustrated. He's never been one to sit around and do nothing. It's driving us all crazy."

"I'll bet. He's lucky he has his family to support him. How's the change to carpenter working for you?"

Lance shrugged. "I always enjoyed the work, but figured I could make more of a difference as a cop. I'm adjusting. We all are."

Lexi tossed her napkin on the table and chuckled. "Tuck is adapting, too. The stories he tells us about his new partner. I think he misses you daily."

His deep voice blended with her feminine one as they laughed together. "He may be afraid to tell me too much so I don't feel guilted into going back."

"You might be right." With a glance at the clock, she stood. "I need to get back."

Lance followed suit and took her tray for her. "Busy day?"

"It usually is in the ER. It's not be-held-at-knife-point busy, but it keeps me hopping."

He returned her bright smile as his mind raced back six months. He and Tuck were working on a case involving the woman who was now Tuck's new bride. Laurie had been stalked by a man searching for information she'd photographed. He stabbed her, but Laurie got a shot off. Later, the man ended up at the ER needing stitches and pain medication. The man found out Lexi had called it in and held her hostage with a knife.

It'd taken every ounce of strength Lance possessed to watch Tuck go through those doors and try to talk the man down while he waited outside.

Thank God the siblings had subdued the guy before he injured Lexi.

Lance called out to her as she started to walk away. "Don't work too hard. I'll see you on Sunday."

She looked over her shoulder, that dark hair caressing her jawline. "Sounds good. Thanks again for lunch."

"Anytime."

He watched her leave, admiring the way she carried herself. Lexi had always appeared certain of who she was and where she was going. It was one of the many things that had drawn Lance to her when they were in high school.

Tuck had known about his infatuation with Lexi, but few others did. Lance said nothing about it at the time because he knew she was leaving for college while he still had two years of high school left to complete. A part of him always regretted not putting himself out there and seeing what would have happened.

That was a long time ago and they were in very different places now.

He tried to shake the woman from his thoughts and headed back to Davenport Carpentry.

Lance slid the heavy wooden door open, the scents of pine and cedar escaping to swirl around him. Minute bits of sawdust floated in the air, illuminated by the ray of sun that cut through it. He inhaled deeply.

Memories vied for his attention. He remembered playing with a wooden train on the floor of the workshop while his dad created a table. Another time, he'd sat on his dad's lap as he helped with the lathe for the first time. The sense of pride and accomplishment when he crafted his first piece all by himself brought a smile to his face. And he'd never forget the happy tears in his mom's eyes when he'd given her the little box with a heart on it for Mother's Day.

There was no way to count how many hours he had clocked watching his dad. Peter had proven time after time he had a true gift and could turn any piece of wood into a work of art.

Thinking about his dad at home, one side of his body weakened from the stroke, made Lance feel sick.

If there was one person who would go insane sitting at home and doing nothing with his hands, it was Peter Davenport.

Lance wandered around the workshop, letting his palm touch the metal of the circular saw.

It had been difficult to leave his job at the Kitner Police Department. But he wasn't about to turn his back on the woodworking business that was part of his family's history.

~

Lexi tried to pull the paper gown down and tuck it under her bare legs. The effort resulted in a small tear in the paper. Yeah, that was helpful.

It was bad enough to sit through the hour-long wait to see her gynecologist, Doctor Yates. The exam and discussion when he arrived lasted all of fifteen minutes. Hardly a fair trade.

Gingerly, she touched her right side. She'd been experiencing pain for months now. Sometimes it would ease up or disappear altogether, but those instances were getting fewer and farther between. What had started out as a twinge had turned into a stabbing ache that made its way into her hip. By the end of the day, she looked forward to relaxing in a hot bath with some Epsom salts. If she tossed in an ibuprofen or two, it usually took the edge off.

This new level of pain convinced her to call the doctor. She figured it was an ovarian cyst that would not go away on its own and she was tired of dealing with the discomfort.

Now she was shivering in the cool air of the room and wondering if she shouldn't have given it more time to resolve on its own. Goodness knows, she had better things to do than freeze to death wrapped up in a paper gown like a slab of meat at the butchers.

Lexi was about to step down from the exam table and get dressed again when there was a light knock on the door. She jumped and made sure the joke of a covering was still tucked in around her when a woman entered the room.

"Alexis Chandler? I'm Tina and I'll be performing your sonogram. Once I've taken images and measurements, I'll have the doctor come in and talk with you."

Lexi nodded. She was glad Doctor Yates would be in to give her his opinion the same day. She had experience reading ultrasound images herself and hoped that she might pick out the ovarian cyst.

Doing her best to remain covered, Lexi scooted down on the bed, lying flat on her back.

Tina asked several questions about her pain before beginning the procedure.

Lexi twisted her head to see the monitor and immediately spotted a dark-colored ring. The tech took measurements and moved the wand around as she manipulated organs to get a better view. Lexi dug her fingernails into the palms of her hand and tried not to whimper at the pain that resulted.

After putting the wand back in its place, Tina stood from her stool. "I'll go get the doctor. He'll want to take a look himself. I'll be right back."

Lexi watched her go and tipped her head back

with a roll of her eyes. The last thing she wanted was to lie on the table any longer than she had to. She rubbed her arms to ward off the goosebumps. Her stomach was a ball of nerves. She wanted to be almost anywhere else right now.

Thankfully, they returned within moments. Tina stood to the side while Doctor Yates sat down on the stool. "I'll take a quick peek here and then I'll elaborate on the findings."

She nodded at him to continue and tried to ignore the dread that was stretching tendrils out to every fiber of her being.

Without watching the monitor, she waited until he had finished and told her she could sit up.

"I know you're a nurse, so I'll come right out and give you the results." He pulled up one of the sonogram photos Tina had taken and tapped the dark ring. "You have a fluid-filled pocket on the anterior side of your right ovary. I wish I could tell you this is a cyst. But here," he circled the white center of the ring, "appears to be a solid mass."

Chapter Two

A mass." Lexi heard herself say the words, but it sounded like they were coming back to her through a tunnel. That her pain was caused by anything more than a stubborn ovarian cyst had never occurred to her. Now she tried to wrap her mind around that idea and it wasn't working.

"Most likely it's benign, but this isn't something you want to assume. It will not go away on its own and it's causing you discomfort." Doctor Yates wrote some notes down in her chart. "At the least, the mass needs to be removed."

Of course it needed to be removed. If there was even a remote chance that the mass wasn't benign, Lexi was tempted to reach in and yank it out herself. She felt betrayed by her own body. She wasn't even thirty years old — whether a mass was malignant or not shouldn't be on her radar. "What do I do?"

"I'm going to refer you to an oncologist. It's better

to go that route because if the doctor gets in there and it isn't benign, you can be sure you're getting the best care."

Oncologist. Ice penetrated her heart. The chill traveled through her blood to every part of her body. She realized Doctor Yates was still talking and forced herself to focus on his words.

"Go ahead and get dressed. I'll come back in with some information." He paused, studying her closely. "Are you okay?"

Lexi stared at her legs, no longer seeing the flimsy paper gown. Minutes ago, covering her legs had been a priority. Now, she felt exposed in an entirely different way. There had been many things she'd taken for granted in her life, including her health.

The doctor was waiting for a response. She nodded and watched as he walked out of the room followed by the technician.

Was she okay?

Not remotely.

She got dressed again, her fingers numb as she tried to smooth the front of her shirt. A twinge in her side made her cringe. She'd always pictured a cyst on her ovary. Now, in her mind's eye, she imagined a nasty little monster clinging to her organ and sucking the life out of her body.

There was a knock on the door and it swung open. Lexi jumped and folded her arms.

Doctor Yates handed her a piece of paper. "Here's the name of the oncologist I'm referring you to. She's in the Dallas area, but it's worth the drive. Her office will call you back this week to schedule an appointment. If you don't hear from them, call them on Monday." He handed her a pamphlet. "This has information about the process you'll be going through to determine what the mass might be. As a nurse, I'm sure you're familiar with all of it and you may have resources where you work that other people might not have access to."

Lexi reached for the information. "I appreciate that."

Five minutes later, she stepped out of the doctor's office and into the sunshine. It was an unseasonably warm summer, and she could feel the heat on her arms. It did little to thaw the chill inside her. Somehow, she managed to put one foot in front of the other until she was enveloped within the safety of her car.

She tossed the information onto the passenger seat. The words at the top of one piece of paper — Cancer Center — seemed to leap off the page. She moved the pages so that it ended up at the bottom and the words were no longer visible.

Her shift at the hospital didn't start until that evening. All of the plans she'd had for the rest of the afternoon seemed trivial.

What was she supposed to do now?

~

The mix of emotions in Lexi's gut were swirling as she pulled up in front of the Chandler house Sunday evening. She had her own apartment in Kitner, but coming here always felt like home.

Until today.

Church had been a blur that morning. She'd tuned everything out and had counted the minutes until she could escape before her family noticed something was wrong.

Lexi sat up straight and glanced at her reflection in the mirror. How could she appear the same on the outside, when everything she knew about her life had changed in the span of a doctor's appointment?

She worked to smooth her hair and get the wayward strands under control. If only she could rein her thoughts in so easily.

She would focus on the welcome home party and get through the evening.

Lexi couldn't wait to see Tuck and Laurie again. It was going to be fun to interact with them as a married couple and to tease them about their honeymoon at a dude ranch. She had every intention of keeping the visit light.

She wasn't about to mention her doctor's visit or that she had an appointment with the oncologist in Dallas the following week. But her family was close and she prayed they wouldn't notice that something was wrong.

The last thing she wanted to do was talk about it and see the expressions on their faces when they got the news.

Taking in a deep breath, Lexi closed her eyes and prayed for strength. God knew she needed a steady spirit and a large dose of courage if she was going to get through tonight.

She reached for the two bags of chips in the passenger seat, straightened her shoulders, and tried to focus on the fact she would be seeing her little brother for the first time in a week.

The thought brought a genuine smile to her face. She clung to that as she approached the front door.

Before she could reach for the knob, it swung

open and her mom, Patty, was smiling at her.

"Come on into the air conditioning, Alexis. It's a hot one today."

Lexi wasn't going to argue with that. It was the final day of August and September promised to be another scorching month.

She was ushered inside with a hug. Goose bumps appeared on her arms as the cool air hit her, but they disappeared just as fast. Her eyes scanned the living room and landed on the tall form near the kitchen.

Tuck glanced up from his conversation with Grams and Laurie to flash that winning smile at her.

They met in the middle, Tuck easily lifting her until her feet no longer touched the carpet. Lexi chuckled. "It's good to see you!"

"You, too. I missed you all."

When Lexi's feet were back on solid ground, she turned to give Laurie a hug as well. "How were the mountains?"

"They were amazing," Laurie responded, her eyes shining. "I'm trying to convince Tuck that we need to buy some property and start a farm."

"She wants to raise goats." Tuck said, intentionally wrinkling his nose. He bumped into his new bride.

"Among other things," she retorted, leaning into his side.

The front door opened again and Lexi heard Lance's voice.

"I wasn't sure whether you two would be here or not." He sat the two bottles of soda and jug of tea down in the kitchen before returning. "I half expected you to call and tell us you'd decided to stay at the dude ranch permanently. Maybe join the rodeo scene."

"If we did that, who would keep you in check?"

Lance threw a punch at Tuck, who expertly deflected it. The men gave each other a bear hug, complete with back pounding.

"Or maybe you need me to keep tabs on you." Lance raised an eyebrow at Tuck.

Lexi shook her head and laughed. The guys had been like this since elementary school and she found the predictability in their friendship to be especially comforting today.

She exchanged a hug with Grams, and little sister, Serenity, when she came in.

"Where's Gideon?"

Serenity motioned to the hallway behind her. "He's finishing up a game. I set a timer for him. He should be out in a few minutes."

Serenity's son, who was turning five in November, had autism. The boy had an amazing ability to focus on the task he was completing, but had a hard time transitioning to something new in certain situations. A timer had been an effective way to help signal to him when it was time to move to a new subject or event.

"How's work going?"

Serenity was employed at Powell Elementary School. Now that it was summer, she was working sporadically. Currently, she was in the middle of a two-week session for children with special needs who benefited from academic help through the summer. She shrugged. "Everything is going well. It's odd to think Gideon will be starting kindergarten over there next fall."

"It'll be a huge blessing for you to be working at the same school he's attending."

"Yes, it will. I'm having a hard time imagining him

ready for school by then. But a lot can happen in a year."

Serenity carried on a polite conversation before she moved off to speak with Lance and Laurie.

Lexi fought back a sigh. Her relationship with Serenity had been nothing but polite since before Gideon was born.

When Serenity had become pregnant with Gideon, her boyfriend left her. Since both of them were teens and immature, Lexi had kept assuring her little sister that once Jay saw the baby, he would change his mind and be a part of their lives. She had built up Serenity's hope.

After Gideon was born, Jay was nowhere to be seen. Serenity tried to contact him and convince him to come see his new son. She never saw her boyfriend again.

As a teen mother who was dealing with a newborn and hormones, Serenity lashed out at her older sister.

Lexi knew that Serenity blamed her for a lot of things. But Serenity had shut her out and refused to talk about it. It only got worse when Gideon was diagnosed with autism.

It hurt that Serenity never did more than carry on a superficial conversation. But there wasn't much Lexi could do, so she hung in there. She hoped that, one day, she could break through the wall that Serenity had placed between them.

The sounds of her family talking broke through her reverie.

Someone had said something that must have embarrassed Laurie because her face was a shade of red that was not unlike her long, curly hair. Tuck put an arm around his bride protectively and tugged her to him, leaning down to kiss her on the temple. Laurie ducked her face into his chest and giggled.

Lexi enjoyed watching the newlyweds interact with each other and with the rest of the family. Thinking of her little brother as a married man would take some getting used to, but it certainly seemed to suit him.

~

Lance ate the last of his second piece of chocolate cake and relaxed in one of the kitchen chairs. He brushed a hand over his goatee to make sure there were no lingering crumbs.

It was good to be at the Chandler house. He'd spent a lot of time there since his childhood. It was like his home away from home.

A movement in the living room caught his attention. He watched as Lexi stood in front of family photos sitting on a shelf. She was observing one of her parents that was taken less than a year before her father had passed away. He thought little of it until he caught her swiping away a tear with one finger.

Instantly alert, Lance excused himself from the conversation and approached her. When she spotted him, he heard her sniff before she turned to face him. She had managed to school her features. He might have imagined the emotion he'd seen moments ago if it weren't for the worry lines at the corners of her mouth.

"Hey, Lance."

"Are you okay?"

"Yep. Is there any cake left?"

The woman had always hated to be the center of

attention. Especially when her own emotions were involved. Lance debated whether he should let it go, but his gut told him to insist. Lexi might be good at hiding her emotions, but he knew something was going on.

"Do you want me to get your mom? Or Tuck?"

"Absolutely not."

The intensity of her response surprised him and only proved he was right.

His thoughts must have shone on his face because Lexi rolled her eyes and exhaled. "Look, Lance. I'm sorry. I'm not about to dampen spirits around here. This is Tuck and Laurie's night. Period."

"There is something wrong, then."

"Let it be."

He watched her walk away. Now what was that about?

Lance enjoyed the welcome home party, but he found his thoughts continued to drift to Lexi. She mostly seemed herself, but her level of enthusiasm appeared forced. No one else noticed, but then most of the focus was on the newly-married couple.

What he didn't miss was that Lexi made a point of not meeting his eyes. The image of one of the strongest women he had ever known wiping away a tear continued to trouble him.

~

Lance put the last coat of paint on a set of two bookcases and stood back to examine them. Satisfied, he placed a lid on the can and used a hammer to seal it closed again.

He had to admit that the business was keeping him

a lot busier than he had anticipated. His dad had built a large customer base. When he could no longer work, Lance half expected many of them to leave. He'd been pleasantly surprised to find they put their trust in him as well. It was a realization that both humbled him and inspired him to live up to the Davenport Carpentry name.

He still missed his career as a police officer. There was something about being able to make an immediate difference in other people's lives. He wasn't sure creating a piece of furniture or repairing a cabinet had quite the same effect.

A life of protecting the residents of Kitner was behind him now. His eyes roamed the workshop, taking in the different projects that awaited his attention. It was time to focus on what was ahead.

Right now, that meant sanding for a while and then shaping new legs for a table set a customer had ordered before his father had the stroke. It was one of the few pieces he had to finish that his dad had originally started.

Lance was so engrossed in his work that when a voice spoke from the entrance to his workshop, he spun around, tool in hand.

"That hammer's almost menacing." There was humor in Lexi's voice.

The bright summer sun shone behind her, creating a silhouette. He might not be able to see her face, but there was no mistaking Lexi's stature. Light shone through the edges of her short hair, illuminating it like a halo.

"If I was worried about who was coming in, I'd have pulled out the real backup." He patted the gun he had concealed at his waist. He'd been carrying a firearm for so many years, it was almost an extension of himself. He had to make a point of going target shooting regularly now that he was no longer with the force.

He put the hammer down and stood.

"Hey, Lex. Come on in."

After dusting the sawdust off the chair in the corner, he motioned to it.

She stepped into the room and he could see her face. Her brown eyes landed on the chair and she crossed her arms. "I'm good, thanks."

He leaned against one of the support beams. "What brings you here?"

Chapter Three

Lexi tried to organize her thoughts. She'd decided to come and apologize after brushing Lance off Sunday night. His concern had been kind and she didn't want him to think she felt otherwise.

He'd been such a frequent visitor to their house growing up that the only way anyone on the outside knew he wasn't a real member of the family was because of his appearance. His blond hair and blue eyes stood in stark contrast to the Chandler family's darker features. He had a goatee he always kept trimmed. She barely remembered him without it.

Lance was studying her, his expression open. Had his eyes always been that intense shade of blue?

A pang of guilt brought her wayward thoughts home. She cleared her throat and tried to think of something to say. "You know, you're the only one who makes a nickname out of my nickname. Is Lexi not short enough for you?"

He chuckled and lifted a shoulder. "For whatever reason, I've always thought 'Lex' in my head since we were kids." He continued to rest against the support beam, his eyes on her.

Come on. Blurt out an apology and be done with it. "Hey, I'm sorry about last night. I hadn't meant to be so rude."

"It's all right. Just because I asked if you were okay didn't mean you had to talk about it. I saw your reaction to that picture of your parents and wanted to check in with you."

"I appreciate that." She paused. "They were happy together. That picture is the last one where my dad looked like himself." Once he'd been diagnosed with pancreatic cancer, his health had degraded rapidly. Much faster than anyone had prepared for. "Thank you for not pushing me."

"I get why you didn't want to go into it last night. Not to mention you have a lot of family I'm sure you turn to first. But I'm here if you need to talk, and I hope you realize that."

"Thanks." She wasn't an overly emotional individual, yet she could feel the tears pricking the back of her eyelids. She closed them, willing the moisture away. Crying in front of Lance was the last thing she wanted to do. "Will you please pray for me on Thursday?" Her voice broke, which frustrated her further.

Lance pushed away from the beam, his brows creased. "Of course I will. You need to talk to your mom or Tuck."

"I can't." She refused to tell them until after her appointment. At two and a half hours away, Dallas wasn't exactly next door. She needed to go through the logistics of the drive and survive the appointment. Once she knew what she was dealing with, she would let her family know.

She hadn't realized her mind had drifted until Lance was beside her and guiding her to the chair.

"I'm worried about you, Lex."

She should have called or sent a note to apologize instead of coming herself. Lexi took a deep breath and was about to stand and leave, but something told her not to. The concern on Lance's face made her pause. "I have to see an oncologist in Dallas on Thursday."

Lance took a step closer and reached for her hand, but stopped before he'd touched her. Thank goodness. She didn't know if she could keep up the calm demeanor if he had.

"I don't want to talk to anyone else until after the appointment. It may be nothing. I won't cause my family worry for no reason."

"But your doctor wants you to see the oncologist just in case."

"Yes."

"What time on Thursday?"

"One in the afternoon."

"And you're going to drive down and back the same day?"

"That's the plan."

Lance gave a quick nod. "I'll take you."

Lexi sprang to her feet. "No, you won't."

"You can't go by yourself. Not to an appointment like this."

She turned away and moved towards the door. "I shouldn't have said anything."

He reached for her arm and stopped her, gently

tugging her around to face him before letting go. The last thing she expected was the warmth his touch created. It spread all the way up her arm and straight to her heart.

"Are you scared?"

Lexi took a steadying breath. "I'd be crazy if I wasn't, right?"

"Yeah, you would. Then I'll pick you up and take you. What time did you plan on leaving?" His eyes dared her to argue with him.

Lexi wanted to object. She wanted to tell him to mind his own business. But she couldn't. Because she didn't want to face the whole thing alone, either. "Eight. I wanted to have time to find the place."

"I'll stop by your apartment at eight on Thursday morning, then."

"Thanks, Lance."

"You're welcome. Do you have my phone number?" She shook her head and he jotted it down on a piece of paper. "If you need anything, or want to talk, call me."

She forced a smile and tucked the paper into a back pocket. "Thanks again. I'll let you get back to work."

Lexi returned to her car and headed for the hospital. The memory of his kindness, and the lingering feel of his hand on her arm, stayed with her the rest of the day.

~

Lance was five minutes from Lexi's place and had spent the majority of the drive in prayer. He hadn't spoken with her since she came to his workshop on

Monday and he had a lot of questions.

What kind of cancer did her doctor suspect? Would they want to perform a biopsy while she was in Dallas?

He'd packed a small bag in case the oncologist surprised her and wanted her to stay the night. They could get two hotel rooms if that were the case.

What would Lexi's prognosis be? That she might have to go through treatment, much less anything worse, tied his stomach in knots.

"God, only You know what our futures hold. No matter what happens today, I pray You fill Lex with wisdom and peace. Please use me as a source of encouragement and strength for her."

He tried to pull his thoughts from the different scenarios that kept running through his mind. There was no sense in going there until she knew more, right?

What if she didn't let him know what the doctor told her today? Then he would have to be content to wait until she felt comfortable sharing the news.

The navy blue Jeep Wrangler he drove had just stopped in front of her apartment when the door swung open. Lance jogged around the vehicle to hold the passenger door for her. He noticed she carried a small duffel bag and offered to put it in the back seat.

They got settled and he drove them through town and onto the highway that lead out of Kitner.

So far, Lexi had said little and he expected a long drive. He glanced at her out of the corner of his eye.

Dressed in dark jeans and a deep purple blouse, she sat with her hands resting on her knees. Her head was up as she watched the terrain speed by. The picture of confidence. That was Lexi.

It had been way too quiet and he tried to think of something to say to spark a conversation. "We'll have to figure out how to get to the doctor's office using the GPS once we get closer to Dallas. Chances are, it's downtown and that area is a mess to drive in."

She nodded. "I have the address. They said to use a big parking structure and take an elevator to the eighth floor. There's a sky bridge that'll lead us over to the right building."

"That sounds like a plan."

They rode in silence which continued to build until it was about all Lance could take. He contemplated turning the radio on.

He had to suppress a start when Lexi cleared her throat.

"I'm not real good about sharing personal things."

"With your brother's friend?"

"With anyone."

He glanced at her and caught a small smile, pulling the corners of his own mouth upwards. "You're the listener."

She angled her head to the side and pursed her lips. "Excuse me?"

"You're the one who listens to everyone else. I remember that was the case when we were kids, too. It seemed like people trusted you with their secrets. But I don't remember you ever talking about yourself much." She was silent and he stole another glance. "Am I wrong?"

"No, you're not wrong."

"Everyone needs to talk things out. I'm not saying you should consider me to be your new best friend. But there's got to be somebody you trust."

Another peek and he could tell she was staring at

him. "I thought you were coming along as my chauffeur, not my priest."

He took a deep breath. The last thing he'd wanted to do was make her angry. But when he saw the twinkle in her eye, a deep laugh rumbled from his chest. "Keep my white collar in the glove box. Check." He gave her a wink and she rewarded him with a smile that lit up her face. He kept his gaze on her for a split second longer before reluctantly returning his attention to the road.

~

Lexi had insisted that Lance go explore the clinic or check out the cafeteria while she waited for her appointment. There was an empty feeling in the pit of her stomach as it was. She didn't need to have him there trying to make her feel better.

He'd agreed, made sure she had his phone number, and disappeared around the corner. She appreciated that he hadn't insisted on staying.

She could see why Tuck and Lance's friendship had lasted into adulthood. There was one thing she could say about the man who drove her here: he was loyal.

Lance was also handsome. The realization surprised Lexi. He wasn't overly tall, but the muscles in his arms were well-defined after years of working for the police force and now as a carpenter. His hands were large, his fingers long. She couldn't help but notice them when he'd stopped her the other day. They were strong, yet had touched her with a gentleness she hadn't expected.

Lexi thought his strongest features were those

bright blue eyes and that disarming smile. When used in combination, she doubted there were many people alive who could resist him.

She felt a measure of guilt for not giving him a proper explanation about her health after all the effort he was putting into helping her. Once she spoke with the oncologist, she would tell him more.

Assuming she ever got called back for her appointment in the first place.

Great, now a muscle near her right eye was twitching. This waiting was going to drive her insane. A peek at the time told her it'd only been five minutes since the last time she'd checked.

If they would call her name before the mass on her ovary plotted to take over the rest of her body, it would be fantastic.

"Alexis Chandler."

She flinched despite the anticipation. Unable to feel her legs, she walked across the room to the nurse holding a door open for her.

"How are you doing today?"

What was she supposed to say? Should she admit she's nervous? Or tell the woman about how this was the last place in the world she wanted to be?

"I'm doing okay. How are you?"

"It's been a busy day around here. I'm going to get your weight and then I'll show you to one of our exam rooms."

Lexi rubbed damp palms on her pants and tried to quiet the pulse that was pounding in her head. She said a silent prayer for God to give her the strength to get through this appointment. She wanted the oncologist to tell her it had all been a mistake and it was just an ovarian cyst after all. She wanted to be all

I'll have several rounds of chemotherapy to make sure it takes care of anything that may have been missed."

She said it matter-of-factly, but he didn't miss that catch in her voice or the tremble in her chin.

"Wow. When are you having the surgery?"

"Two weeks from today."

Lance leaned back against his chair and let out a slow lungful of air. What was he supposed to say to her? That it would all be okay? That she wouldn't have to deal with the chemo because it was benign?

He couldn't. Not honestly. But there was one thing he could tell her.

"You're resilient, Lex. No matter what happens, you're going to power through. You have a lot of people who will be there to support you. I'll be praying that God will give you the strength you need."

"How am I going to tell my family about this? My dad's battle with pancreatic cancer was nasty. It nearly destroyed my mom. I can't put her through this again."

For the first time since she had come out of the office, Lexi's eyes held a hint of the panic she felt. She massaged her temple with a finger and shut her eyes.

"Patty will be okay. This is different. You aren't your dad. You guys made it through before as a family, and you'll make it through this." He reached across the table and covered her hand with his own. Her skin was softer than he could have imagined. The discovery threatened to derail his thoughts. "If you need anything, please let me know."

She nodded, her eyes fixed on the fry still propped up in the ketchup. "I appreciate that. You did a lot driving me here. You were right to insist I not come alone."

Lance moved his hand from hers and instantly missed the warmth. "I wish I'd recorded that. Alexis Chandler admitted I was right. That doesn't happen often."

Lexi pointed a finger at him. "Don't expect to hear it again from me anytime soon."

He realized that when she teased, there was a little crinkle at the outside corners of both of her eyes. He found it alluring.

She popped the nearly-forgotten fry in her mouth. "This food is awesome."

"I'll get you a meal and sneak it into you at the hospital after your surgery."

She lifted her head in time to catch his wink and answered it with a smile. "You would, too, wouldn't you?"

"You can count on it."

~

Lance turned as the door to his workshop opened and admitted a tall, lanky man who cast a look around the room.

"Can I help you?"

"Hi. My name is Donald Karr." He reached out to shake Lance's hand. "I'm here to pick up some custom barstools my wife ordered."

"Sure. Let me grab those for you."

Lance retrieved the barstools along with the invoice. The woman who'd come in had found a single barstool she liked at a yard sale. She brought it in to see if he could recreate two more just like it. The barstool itself wasn't particularly ornate, though it had been a challenge for Lance. He'd been happy with the end result. As always, however, it came down to what the customer thought.

He set the barstools in front of Donald and indicated the first one. "This is the original. I repainted it so that all three matched, as per the agreement." Lance waited while Donald inspected them.

"These are fantastic. You did great work here. My wife will love these." He checked the invoice, pulled his wallet out, and handed Lance his debit card.

Lance gave a crisp nod. "I'll go run this and be right back with your receipt." When he returned, he helped Donald load the furniture into the back of his pickup. They used an old blanket to protect them from any damage during transport.

Donald held a hand out and shook Lance's. "Thanks again."

"You're welcome. I appreciate your business."

Lance watched him leave and grinned. He whistled as he got back to work. Seeing a customer pleased with something he'd crafted with his own two hands was like a natural high. To know that the family would use that furniture for years to come made it even better.

No wonder his dad enjoyed his work so much.

~

Lexi had dreaded this for days.

It'd been hard enough to act like herself at church that morning. Praise and worship had gone a long way in giving her the peace she craved, but knowing what she would tell her family that evening had her stomach in knots.

Lance had gone to the same church as her family for years. This Sunday, he asked if he could take the seat next to her and she'd nodded her agreement. Having someone else there that shared her secret helped give her the strength she needed to make it through the service. When it was over and everyone was leaving, he leaned closer to her ear and whispered, "I'm praying for you tonight."

Now she was trying to relax at the Chandler house, but her family knew her too well. They hadn't even gotten through the meal before her mom had thrown looks of concern across the table. Tuck questioned whether she was feeling okay.

Apparently, she wasn't as good at pretending all was well as she would've liked to think.

Lexi could feel all eyes on her as she took a deep breath. She couldn't put it off any longer. Reaching deep, she cleared her throat and told them all about her appointments.

Patty covered her mouth with her hand, blinking quickly as tears filled her eyes. Grams clutched the compass locket that Gramps had given her many years ago. Her lips were moving and Lexi knew she was praying.

Tuck looked like he was ready to tackle something while Laurie moved to put an arm around Lexi's shoulder and gave her a squeeze.

Her eyes fell on Serenity, who sat at the kitchen table and seemed to study everything else in the room.

Lexi felt like she was suffocating under the emotional weight of the moment. "Come on, guys. I'm having surgery. We don't even know for sure it's cancer. You're making me feel like I'm on my deathbed."

Grams joined Laurie and went to stand on the other side of Lexi. She put an arm around her granddaughter. "She's right. Together, we pray. We pray that the doctor has wisdom and that the tumor is benign. And we'll continue to pray every step of the way."

Lexi let herself lean into the older woman and soak up all the strength she could. "Thanks, Grams."

Patty went forward and hugged Lexi tightly while Tuck gave her a reassuring nod.

Movement at the doorway captured Lexi's attention. Gideon stood there, his eyes flitting from one person to the other. After a moment, he walked forward to put his little arms around as many people as he could.

That had all of them laughing as they moved to include him in what had ended up being a group hug. Lexi knew he didn't understand what they'd discussed before the giant show of affection, which made the boy's hug all the sweeter.

~

When Lexi spotted Lance in the cafeteria the following week, her mood improved tenfold. Once he'd seen her, he got up and chose something for lunch.

They met again at the table, slid into their chairs, and began to eat.

"Do you keep a schedule of the cafeteria meals on your fridge at home?"

Lance chuckled. "No, on the bulletin board at the

shop." He raised an eyebrow at her and she wasn't sure whether or not he was kidding.

"And do you like Mexican food, too?"

"I like almost any kind of food." He jabbed his enchilada. "Though today, they are pushing my envelope a bit."

It was her turn to laugh now. "It does look a little like rubber." She took a bite out of one of her tacos and pointed to it. "Stick with the basics. It's safer." She studied him over her plate. "What brought you all the way over here today?"

"I wanted to see how you were doing. Tuck said Sunday night went well. I imagine it was still a huge shock to your family."

"It was. But they all handled it pretty well. I'm just glad that's over. I was dreading it and I think the apprehension was worse than the night itself." She paused, giving him a small smile. "And I'm doing okay. Thank you for asking."

Lance took another bite of rice and pushed it to the side of his plate. "I'm glad." He laid his fork down. "I was thinking about your surgery. I'd like to be there. I wanted to make sure you were okay with that and it didn't make you feel uncomfortable."

His words wrapped around Lexi like a soft blanket. She liked the idea of Lance being there while she was in surgery. "I appreciate that. Thank you."

A slow smile spread across his face and his blue eyes fastened on her. "Good."

"You could have called and asked me. You didn't have to make a special trip for the mediocre Mexican food."

"I don't think you've officially given me your phone number. I didn't want to stalk."

Lexi snorted in an un-lady-like fashion and covered her mouth with her napkin. "We've known each other forever, Lance. I remember when you and Tuck destroyed my POG collection. I wouldn't consider a phone call from you to be stalking."

Lance had the good sense to appear embarrassed. "I always felt bad about that. We didn't set out to ruin your entire collection. They were perfect for setting fire to with magnifying glasses. In retrospect, we should have moved the rest of the collection away from the burn zone." He stroked his goatee, a sheepish smile on his face. "If it helps, my dad grounded me for a week because I was careless with fire."

"That helps a little." Laughing, she got a card out of her billfold and handed it to him. "Now you have my phone number. Officially and all that."

He tipped his head and smiled. "Thank you."

They spent the rest of their lunch making fun of some of the other phases they'd gone through as kids before going back to work again.

~

The night before her surgery, Lexi stared at the hotel ceiling and sighed. She'd been trying to sleep for hours with no luck.

Checklists kept popping up in her mind. She'd gotten everything squared away at the hospital in Kitner and would return to work in a week — possibly less. All of that assuming, of course, that she didn't have to have a hysterectomy.

She'd shared her situation with Kate and made her promise to keep the details to herself. If everything went Lexi's way, there was no sense in alarming her coworkers. She was having a minor surgery and that's all they needed to know.

Patty and Grams had taken their nervous energy and focused it on cooking. Over the last few days, they'd managed to stock her freezer with all kinds of easy meals that Lexi could reheat when she got hungry.

She had to be at the hospital in five hours. All she needed to do in the morning was get dressed and make sure everything had made it back into her duffel bag.

There was a noise at the door. Lexi held her breath. When she heard it again, it sounded more like a knock. She slipped out of bed and padded over to it, peeking through the peep hole. Her mom was standing outside. She released the locks and opened the door.

"You can't sleep either, huh?" Patty gave Lexi a hug.

"My mind won't give me a chance." Lexi sat on the edge of the bed and Patty joined her. "Every time I relax and start to fall asleep, my brain plays the 'What if' game. What if they can't remove the mass? What if it's worse than they think? What if I have to have a hysterectomy?"

Patty's eyes were filled with tears. "Oh sweetie, I'm sorry you're going through this."

"I'm sorry you are, too, Mom. After everything with Dad, you shouldn't have to be dealing with this again. It's not fair." She balled up her fist, squeezing as tightly as she could. "Getting cancer wasn't my fault. Still, I can't help but wonder if there were some foods I should have avoided, or vitamins I could have taken to strengthen my immune system."

"Shoulda. Woulda. Coulda. They're dangerous words, Alexis. And none of them do you a bit of good."

"I know." She did, too. Every time her mind tried to go off on a tangent, she did her best to pull it back and focus on the task at hand. She prayed again for strength and for peace — something she'd been doing every time she felt her courage start to slip. She glanced at the clock on the nightstand. "Grams will miss you."

Patty and Grams had decided to share a hotel room to cut down on cost. "She was awake, too. I told her I was coming over to check on you."

Lexi nodded. "I hope Gideon's doing okay in the hotel tonight. I'm worried about Serenity. She won't talk to me."

"Don't take it personally. She's not talking to any of us about your surgery. I think there's something she's struggling with right now. I don't know if it's because of the way we lost your dad, or if it's another issue completely. When she's ready, she'll let us know."

"You're probably right." Lexi leaned over and let her head rest against Patty's shoulder. "I love you, Mom."

"I love you, too, Alexis."

They visited for another half hour before Lexi insisted Patty go back to her room and at least try to get some sleep before the surgery.

When she bid her mom a good night, Lexi retrieved a tablet from her bag, pulled the comforter off the bed, and curled up on the small plush chair in her room. If sleep wasn't going to happen, she could at least have one of her favorite books to occupy her mind until the sun came up.

Chapter Five

Lexi changed into the gown the nurse had given her and tried to get comfortable on the hospital bed. She nodded that she was ready and Patty went to open the door. The rest of the family gathered around her bed, Lance coming in right behind them.

Gideon was squinting, his eyes riveted to the floor at his feet. He was calm, which said a lot since he rarely did well in medical settings. Squinting like that was his way of handling a situation that was visually overwhelming to him.

She smiled at him. "Hey, Gideon. Thanks for coming to see me."

He turned his head to look at her, his eyes little slits. Serenity tightened an arm around his shoulder and gave Lexi a tentative smile. "He's worried about you."

"I'm good, buddy. You don't need to worry about

me." She moved her right arm to hide the IV as best she could. "I'm more than ready to get this ball rolling, though. Is it cold in here, or is it just me?"

Patty produced a blanket and spread it out over Lexi's form.

"Thanks, Mom." The blanket did little to help and she realized it had to be her nerves that were prompting her shivers. Her eyes roamed the room, pausing at each of the people who had taken time to come and see her: Patty, Grams, Tuck, Laurie, Serenity, Gideon, and Lance. She received smiles, nods, winks, and thumbs up. "You all didn't have to come, but I appreciate it."

Tuck held Laurie's hand with one of his and elbowed his best friend in the ribs with the other. "If you have any trouble back there, let us know, and we'll come in with guns blazing."

"In a heartbeat," Lance agreed.

"I have no doubt you guys would do that, too. Don't worry, I'll call if I need the cavalry."

The door opened and the doctor entered followed by the anesthesiologist and a nurse.

Lexi listened as they again explained what would happen in surgery. They wanted to see if she had any questions. When she assured them she didn't, the anesthesiologist stepped forward.

"I'm going to start medication in your IV to make you sleepy. You'll still be awake when we get to the operating room, but you're not likely going to remember it."

She held up a hand to stop him. "I'm a registered nurse. I know the drill."

"In that case, stop me if you need anything."

"You got it."

Lexi leaned back against her pillow and felt the sting as the medication entered her body through the IV, followed by warmth as it traveled through her blood stream.

Grams stepped forward to take her hand. "Let's pray." When everyone had bowed their heads, she began. "Our heavenly Father, we ask that you surround Lexi with Your perfect love and peace. We pray for clear minds and wisdom for the doctors and nurses who will be performing this surgery. We pray that you place an angel in that operating room to give guidance to all involved. We ask that Your will be done."

Several murmurs of agreement echoed in the small room followed by a moment of silence before Tuck closed the prayer.

"Thank you for carrying Your children through the challenges in life and for Your faithfulness. In the name of Jesus, Your Son, we pray, amen."

"Amen."

The word was uttered by the rest of the family in unison. The nurse and the anesthesiologist prepared her bed for transport. "We'll take good care of her," the nurse assured them.

Lexi's eyelids were getting heavy as the nurse wheeled her out of the room and into the hallway.

~

Lance listened as Patty told the story of Tuck when he had his appendix removed as a child.

"The doctors warned us he shouldn't eat much for the rest of the day. But you know Tuck, he's always hungry — and he eats a lot."

Tuck groaned and Laurie patted his knee sympathetically, a smile on her face.

"She's never let me live this down. I was seven."

His mother chortled as she continued. "He was resting on the couch and we were keeping an eye on him. The next thing we know, he's in the kitchen eating a sandwich and diving into a bag of chips. How the boy moved that swiftly after a surgery, I still don't know."

Laurie shook her head and gave Tuck's leg a squeeze. "You didn't."

He shrugged. "I did. I had convinced myself I was starving to death."

Patty pointed at him. "And what the doctor predicted came true — you wound up sick as a dog, on top of having an incision."

"One of the most painful moments of my childhood." Tuck placed a hand on his side. "I can honestly say that sandwich, no matter how good it tasted at the time, wasn't worth it."

Grams' laughter blended with the others. "It doesn't surprise me. You never had a strong stomach. Not like Lexi. She takes after me. Our stomachs are made out of iron." She shifted her legs and crossed her ankles as she prepared to tell her story.

Lance thought back to the discussions that went on in his own family and they weren't unlike this one.

Laurie seemed to enjoy every single one of them. He knew that she hadn't had much of a childhood and she appeared to find the Chandler stories entertaining.

He checked his watch. Lexi had been in surgery for just over an hour. The doctor said it could take as little as an hour and as long as three, it would depend

She smiled, a twinkle lighting her tired, brown eyes. "Thanks, Lance. I think I'll be okay. I'm going to eat a chicken strip or two, set up a blockade to prevent the nurses from bothering me, and pass out for the duration of the night."

He knew she was kidding, but he could picture her limping to the door and finding a way to bar it closed. "Well, don't overdo it. I'll see you soon, I'm sure."

"I'm sure. Drive careful."

Lance lifted his hand in farewell and left the room, closing the door softly behind him. As he walked to his car, all he could think about was Lexi. He pictured the way her dark hair had fanned out over her pillow. The woman had an amazing ability to face a difficult situation with her head up. He admired that about her. But as determined as she was, everyone could see she was in pain. If circumstances were different, he'd have sat with her through the night.

As he drove down the highway towards his hometown, he replayed the day's events in his head.

"God, thank you for watching over Lex today. Thank you for guiding the hands of the doctors, that they were able to remove all the cancer. I pray that you give her peace so she can rest and recover as fast as possible." He paused. "Please let the chemotherapy coming up do its job and get rid of this cancer for good."

Because a world without Alexis Chandler wasn't a reality he cared to consider.

~

Lance slid into one side of the booth across from Tuck. They had made arrangements to meet for breakfast that Monday morning before their work days began. They used to do that regularly when he worked with Tuck and it was one of the things he missed the most. Sometimes, Lance wished he had more people around during business hours. By evening, he often felt starved for conversation.

He figured it would get better with time. But for now, he missed regular visits with his best friend.

They both ordered steak, eggs, and toast. Once their food arrived, they wasted no time in digging in.

Lance raised an eyebrow. "Doesn't Laurie feed you?"

Tuck swallowed and held a hand up. "Oh, she cooks fine. Better than fine. But she's a little more into light breakfasts. Which I have no problem with. I'm just enjoying the steak and eggs."

"Gotcha. They do taste good. We should meet here once a week."

"We should."

Five minutes later, they had agreed to have breakfast together every Monday morning. A good way to help kick off a new week.

When their meals were gone, Lance leaned back in his seat. "How's Lexi feeling?"

"She's doing well, considering. She stayed with Mom Friday night and Saturday, but decided she wanted to go home on Sunday."

Lance chuckled. "That doesn't surprise me at all. When is her post-op appointment?"

He knew she would find out about the chemotherapy then. The thought of it turned his stomach into knots. He could only imagine how Lexi was dealing with the wait for more information.

"It's this Friday." Tuck finished his glass of milk.

"She doesn't want it to be a big thing and is insisting she would drive herself if the doctor hadn't put restrictions on her. Doctor Ravenhill told her ten to fourteen days. Lexi said she's tempted to push it and drive herself anyway. We're still working on convincing her to let someone go with her. I think she's going to be in pain after her appointment."

Lance nodded, his mind racing. He didn't like the idea of Lexi going by herself, either. "I'll be praying she changes her mind about that."

"I appreciate it. She's independent and she thinks she has to spare everyone the worry. But what she needs is to accept help from other people right now."

~

Lexi was lounging on her futon, re-runs of *Diagnosis Murder* playing on the television. It was a show she'd liked for years, but one could only take lying around watching it for so long.

She was a nurse. She knew full well it was going to take a while to recover from a complete hysterectomy. She wanted to be as healthy as possible when she began chemotherapy, but it didn't mean she wouldn't go insane in the process.

All this down time had given her plenty of time to do research since her surgery.

Chemotherapy scared her with each side effect she read about. It inspired her to look up some of the alternative cancer treatments as well as ways to help reduce the intensity of the side effects themselves.

There were many other options that people claimed eliminated their cancer without the need for damaging radiation or chemotherapy. These treatments ranged from eating special diets and vitamins to herbs and oils.

Lexi had been praying about the options and hadn't felt a strong leaning in either direction.

Unless that changed, she planned on having chemo, but doing many of the natural treatments as well. Worst case scenario, they do nothing. But she hoped that they would at least build up her immune system. Best case scenario, they help to eliminate the cancer cells that might still invade her body.

She had a book full of notes and had located several health food stores in the Dallas area. Lexi planned on checking them out when she went for her post-op appointment on Friday.

A tone announced a text and she stretched to retrieve her cell phone from the coffee table. The effort made her draw back as muscles objected.

A smile appeared when Lance's name came up. "How are you doing today?"

He had sent her a text every day since her hysterectomy. She responded and they conversed back and forth a few times.

"I'm okay. Tired of doing nothing. How are you?" she texted back.

"Busy day but good. Can I bring you lunch?"

On one hand, having another living person there to visit with sounded wonderful. On the other, she felt like a complete mess and was in desperate need of a shower.

But the requirement for food and company won out and she typed back, "That would be awesome. Thank you!"

"Great! If tacos work for you, I'll bring them by at noon."

"I never say no to tacos. See you then!"

That gave her an hour and a half to get moving a little and at least get cleaned up.

Chapter Seven

Lance knocked on the door to Lexi's apartment, a large bag of food in one hand. He hadn't known whether he was dropping it off, or joining her for lunch. Unable to think of a way to ask without putting pressure on her to invite him in, he opted to buy extra food. That way, there would be plenty either way. She could always eat some of it later.

"It's open!"

Her voice filtered through the wooden door. He turned the knob and pushed it open with his elbow.

"You know, you should keep your door locked and make sure you know who's there before you invite him in," he teased.

"I saw you park through the window and unlocked the door afterwards. I knew it was you."

Had she been waiting for him to arrive? More likely, it was a coincidence that she saw him while catching a glimpse outside. Still, the thought made him smile.

He spotted her sitting on the futon, her feet propped up on the coffee table. She was wearing a maroon running suit and her hair was damp. She smiled brightly as he gave her a wave.

"You're sitting up, that's a good sign."

She shrugged. "I've been lying down a lot. It's nice to have a minor change in scenery. I can almost see the dust on the top of my TV from this elevation."

Lance chuckled as he sat on the opposite end. It had been hard to see her tired and in pain at the hospital. That sparkle in her eyes was a relief.

"I know you like tacos, but figured you might want a variety. You can eat what you like and put the rest in the fridge until later."

He withdrew tacos, fajitas, nacho cheese, chips, and a couple of burritos.

Lexi's eyes grew wide. "Wow. Yeah, that should keep me in food for days. I don't suppose you have time to stay and eat. Don't get me wrong. I enjoy listening to Dick Van Dyke talk as much as the next girl. But he doesn't give me much of a chance to get a word in edgewise and that's putting a damper on our relationship."

With a laugh, he handed her a napkin. "I would be more than happy to stay and eat with you. Do you have any plates?"

"In the cabinet above the sink. There's not much to drink in the fridge except for water and iced tea."

"I've got it handled."

He found what he needed in the kitchen and returned, setting up their lunch spread on the coffee table. He asked what she wanted and filled her plate, handing it, a paper towel, and a glass of tea to her.

"Thank you."

Lance watched as she settled the plate on her lap. He followed suit and soon they were enjoying their Mexican food in comfortable silence.

Lexi finished her first taco and brushed crumbs off her mouth with the paper towel. "Tuck said you guys got to have breakfast yesterday."

"Yeah, it was nice. Between my job change and him being a newly married man, we haven't had a lot of opportunities to get together and hang out."

"I'm sure. He misses you at work. But I've never seen him happier than he is now with Laurie."

Lance thought about his best friend and couldn't agree more. Marriage suited him. He knew that Tuck had spent a long time convinced he would never find the right woman for himself. Lance thought back to the first time they'd met Laurie. Tuck had fallen fast and hard for the photographer.

He must have been smiling at the memories because Lexi was watching him, a grin on her face. "What are you thinking about?"

"How Laurie turned Tuck into a giant puppy dog."

She tipped her head back and laughed hard. "She did at that. I wouldn't tell him that to his face, though."

Lance winked at her. "He's big, but he's not as fast as I am."

He and Tuck had wrestled for fun a lot growing up. He remembered one instance when the two of them had been racing in the Chandler backyard. They were twelve. Lance had caught Tuck and tackled him to the ground. Lexi had rolled her eyes, mumbling something about boys before turning around and

Time with her was quickly unearthing his feelings and bringing them into the light. A fact he was well aware of and, at the moment, had no clue what to do with.

~

Lexi accepted a hug from Grams and then another from Patty. The women had come by to see if she needed anything before her appointment on Friday.

"I'm glad you're going to let Lance drive you," Patty was saying as Grams perused the contents of her refrigerator. "I still wish you'd let me take you instead, though."

"Mom, I appreciate it. I don't want you to go through all of this again." Lexi glanced at the kitchen. "What are you doing in there, Grams?"

"Honey, you could use more to drink in here. Your mom and I will go by the store and get you juice and more tea. Is there anything else you'd like?"

Lexi wrinkled her nose and shook her head. "You guys don't need to go to the store for me. I'm fine here."

Patty gave her a firm look. "You know Grams. Once she's decided to do something, you can't sway her. And if I can't take you to your appointment, I want to help in another way."

The moisture in Patty's eyes, and seeing Grams standing in the doorway with her hands on her hips, forced Lexi's surrender. "That would be great, thank you both."

Grams dug around in her purse for a piece of paper and a pen. She handed them to Lexi. "Write out a list for us and we'll get everything you need."

She did as she was told, adding several things to the small scrap. Besides a few items for the kitchen, she included shampoo, lotion, and socks. When she was done, she handed it back to Grams.

Patty scanned it over her shoulder. "What kind of socks do you need?"

Lexi shrugged. "Something fun. My feet have been cold ever since my surgery and I'm tired of wearing the gray and black socks I have here. Colors. Cartoon characters. Anything's good."

After they left, Lexi called Kitner Memorial Hospital and spoke with Kate. She wanted to find out how everything was going in her absence. She told her friend about the cancer but asked her to not say anything to anyone else.

"I'll tell people if I need to once I get back."

Kate promised to keep the details to herself.

Lexi took a short nap.

When they returned, Patty put the drinks in the fridge before carrying another bag over to the futon. She and Grams sat down and pulled the contents out.

Patty held up a pack of six socks in solid, neon colors. "These are for when you want to wear something a little tamer."

"Those are tame?!" Lexi giggled.

Grams gave her a wink. "Compared to these," she said, handing her two pairs that had toes in them with rainbow colors striped all the way up.

"Or these." Patty gave her a pair of socks with suns all over them and another pair covered in red hearts.

Lexi was getting a kick out of the footwear. "These are all awesome, thank you." She put an arm around each of them, drawing them to her in a hug. "I appreciate you. I hope you guys know that."

"We love you, Alexis." Patty stroked her daughter's cheek. "You come from a line of strong women. Lean on us when you need to, huh?"

"I love you, too." Her heart full, she blinked back tears. "Okay, enough of this mushy stuff." She picked up a pair of the toed, rainbow socks. "I have to try these on right now."

Chapter Eight

L exi had kept herself focused and composed through the entire post-surgical appointment. She'd brought a notebook and pen, writing down everything the oncologist said. It was way too much to remember at the time and she figured she could parse it out later if she needed to.

She was thankful Doctor Ravenhill was more than patient as she answered all of Lexi's questions.

The physical exam of her incision was the most painful part of the visit. The doctor was as careful as she could be, but it was still uncomfortable. Pressure to that area gave her a similar physical reaction to the one she had when she heard the sound of fingernails on a chalkboard.

"Your incision is healing well. I'm going to clear you to drive as long as you feel okay. But you still need to watch your activity for another few weeks. Those muscles will take a while to heal. The most important thing to remember is to listen to what your body is telling you. In general, it can take up to six weeks before you start feeling like yourself again."

Doctor Ravenhill then talked about her treatment.

An hour later, Lexi clutched her notebook under one arm and made her way back out to the waiting room. Lance approached her.

"Are you all right?"

She gave him a short nod. "Yeah. I'm done." She glanced at her watch. "I didn't realize it, but she is sending me over to the cancer center for my first of three chemotherapy sessions."

Lance's eyebrows flew upward. "Right now?"

"Yep."

He wavered a moment before taking charge and she was happy to let him. "Let's figure out where we're supposed to go next."

~

They found their destination easily. The cancer center was situated just two miles from the hospital. As Lance watched Lexi check in and then wait to be called back, the only thing he knew to do was pray.

When they called her name, she stood and hesitated, glancing behind her.

"I can come back with you if you'd like."

She gave him a firm nod. They followed the nurse into the room on the other side.

The nurse showed Lexi to a chair that reminded Lance of a mix between a dentist's chair and an expensive recliner. It had a raised section for the legs and the part at the upper back and head could be raised and lowered depending on what she needed or preferred.

He waited as she took a seat and then the nurse surprised him by bringing a chair over for him. "Thank you."

"This process takes a while. You may as well be comfortable."

Lance sat and listened as they explained everything to Lexi. They inserted an IV, said she could push a button to call if she needed anything, and someone would be back to check on her in a while.

Lexi's dark lashes kissed her cheeks when she closed her eyes. She breathed in and out deliberately. "Nothing like the feel of poison being pumped into the veins to relax a person."

He wasn't sure if he should laugh, groan, or pull the IV out of her arm. He hadn't realized he'd been staring at the bag containing the medication when her hand touched his.

"Hey, you're way too serious, there."

"I'm sorry." His eyes went to their hands. Without allowing time to talk himself out of it, he turned his hand over to cradle hers. "I hate you're having to go through this."

Lexi seemed surprised by his motion, but didn't say anything. She left her hand in his. "If I had known they were going to have me do this first session today, I would have had someone else bring me."

"Why?"

"I hate being seen like this."

"By me specifically? Or anyone in general?"

She raised her eyebrow and withdrew her hand. He wished he'd kept his mouth shut.

"They told me this could take up to three hours. Feel free to leave and I can come find you when I'm done."

Lance shook his head. "Not on your life. I'm staying right here." His voice sounded husky, even to himself. He could still feel the weight of her hand in his. No, he wasn't going anywhere, not while she was sitting in a cancer center, an IV in her arm.

Tuck had it all wrong. Lance didn't have feelings for Lexi like he did when they were teens.

This was much more.

He was in love with Lexi.

Maybe he always had been.

His heart thundered in his chest as his mind struggled to comprehend exactly what that meant.

Watching the woman he loved go through this made him feel powerless when all he wanted to do was fix the world for her. If he could, he would take her place right now.

His gaze was still on her hand. When it moved to her face, there was a flash of recognition in her eyes that rapidly switched to apprehension.

~

Lance brushed her arm with a finger. "There's nothing for you to worry about." He leaned back, his chair squeaking in protest.

The expression on Lance's face a moment ago had been so intense, that it almost scared Lexi. Between that and the way he'd held her hand, she had a flashback to when they were in school. She'd known he had a crush on her, but had been really good at ignoring it. There was no way he still had feelings for her after all this time. If there was even a possibility that he did, this needed to be the last time he brought her for a session. She didn't want him to get the wrong idea.

She'd seen Lance around Gideon enough to know he would be an amazing dad someday. He deserved a family with children of his own.

Most men, when they're ready to settle down, want the whole package. Thanks to her hysterectomy, that was one thing she could never give a husband.

It was something she'd been wrestling with a lot lately. Lexi was relieved that the cancer was removed. She would rather live a long, healthy life than be able to have a child of her own someday.

At the same time, it was hard to not feel less than whole.

Lance may not have thought about it yet, but she had no doubt that not having children of his own would become an issue someday.

She was desperate to shake the thoughts from her head. None of this mattered because she was reading emotions into him that weren't there in the first place. Right?

"How's your dad doing?"

"He's good." He sat forward, his elbows on his knees. He seemed to be relieved at the change in topic. "Mom's trying to find a new hobby for him. She keeps suggesting things to him or offering to sign him up for classes. He hasn't been interested. I think he feels lost right now. He lived his life in that carpentry shop."

"I bet it's hard. What other interests does he have?"

"My parents used to attend renaissance festivals. They would spend all year planning their outfits and Dad would make things to sell there."

"Given the names of you and your sisters, that somehow doesn't surprise me."

He laughed. "That was where my dad took her on their first date."

"When was the last time they went to a renaissance festival?"

"It's been a few years. We used to go every year to a big one in Oklahoma when my sisters and I were kids. I guess, once we grew up, they didn't go anymore." Lance appeared thoughtful as he leaned back. "That's brilliant. Maybe, if we can get him to the festival this year, it'll inspire him. There were a lot of things he liked about it. If nothing else, it'll be a good distraction."

"There you go!" Lexi had only met Lance's parents a handful of times, but they had both seemed genuinely kind. "That sounds like fun. Maybe you can contact your sisters and get everyone to go together as a family again. After what happened to your dad, they might welcome the chance to spend time with him anyway."

"They might. I'll call them tomorrow. Marian is six months along with her fourth child. I would be surprised if they could come. But I'm hoping the others will be able to make it."

She watched as he seemed to mull things over. She let him take his time. After a glance at the clock, she closed her eyes a few minutes to let them rest.

The next thing Lexi knew, a sound seemed to echo in her head. Her eyes flew open as she tried to locate the source of the noise. She found Lance watching her, a tender expression on his face.

"Did I fall asleep?"

"Yes. It was only for fifteen minutes. You must

have needed it, though."

"I didn't get much last night."

"I don't blame you. But you're nearly two-thirds done with this first session."

Lexi looked down at her arm where they had placed the IV. She flexed her hand, the tape pulling on her skin. "I'm ready to be done. Next time, I'll come prepared with a book. Or two. Oh, and a sandwich."

"At this rate, it'll be five at the earliest before we're back in Kitner. If you're not feeling up to it, let me know. We can get two hotel rooms and go home in the morning."

"I'm sure it'll be fine."

"I don't mind. Tuck mentioned it might be better if you did take it easy. Once we're back, you can always call someone to stay with you until you know what kind of side effects you might experience."

Lexi tried to tamp down her impatience. It seemed like all everyone had done since she'd told them about her cancer was treat her like she couldn't take care of herself. It was maddening!

She willed herself to hold her tongue, but the combination of lack of sleep and stress made her efforts futile.

"Do me a favor and let Tuck know that I'm not an invalid. I'll go home, I'll take care of myself, and I'll be back to work in a week." It had come out much harsher than she intended.

Lance's eyebrows shot upwards. "Because having people who love you is a bad thing. There's a huge difference between trying to help because someone is worried about you versus thinking you're an invalid. I think you should give your family more credit than that."

Zing. That stung.

She made a fist with her free hand and closed her eyes.

He was right.

"I'm sorry." Her voice was little above a whisper. "I know I'm being oversensitive. I'm the one who takes care of everybody else and it's always been that way. In case it isn't obvious, I don't like relying on other people. Being weak like this is frustrating me."

She opened her eyes, half expecting to see Lance angry. Or maybe even shaking his head with pity.

The admiration he projected had not even been on the list.

"Lex. You aren't weak. You're one of the strongest women I've ever known. And you are going through a lot." He paused. "I shouldn't have said what I did. I apologize."

Boy, he was full of surprises today.

"No. You were right to call me out on that. I admit I may be feeling sorry for myself right now. In more ways than one."

Lance moved a hand towards her but put it back on his knee. "I'm here if you need to talk. And it's not like we don't have plenty of time."

A sharp pain in her temple caused her to grimace. She brought an index finger up to massage it.

"Are you okay? Should I get the nurse?"

"It's been a long day." She shifted her position in the chair.

Lance nodded at her feet. "Those are awesome, by the way."

Lexi realized he had noticed her socks. She lifted her pants leg a little to show off the bright yellow suns. "Mom and Grams bought me a bunch. I decided I was going to wear some of the loudest whenever I go to an appointment or I'm feeling a little down. They make me smile."

"That's a great idea. I'm sure they'll get a kick out of knowing you're wearing them today."

"I guess I should text everyone and let them know what's happening, shouldn't I?"

"It might not be a bad idea." He took her phone from the side pocket of her bag and handed it to her.

~

Lexi insisted on going back home after her chemotherapy session. She seemed to feel okay and Lance didn't argue with her.

The sun was setting when he took her by the apartment and walked her to the door.

"If you need anything, please call someone. It takes a strong person to admit when he or she needs help." A breeze blew some hair into her face. He couldn't resist and reached out to swipe away a few strands from her cheek.

"I can't begin to thank you for being with me today. You helped make an overwhelming situation a little more manageable." Her brown eyes focused on her hands that she held clasped in front of her.

When they rose to meet his, the vulnerability that pooled there made him wish cancer were a man that he could find and beat to a pulp.

It also gave him an intense desire to pull her into his arms and protect her from all the bad in the world.

Unable to resist, he took her hand in his and drew

her into an embrace. Her arms went around his waist as she leaned into his hug. The scents of lavender and citrus surrounded him as her hair fluttered like a butterfly against his face.

"You're my super hero, Lex."

She gave him a little squeeze in response.

Lance leaned back enough to gaze into her face. He softy traced the outline of her jaw with a finger and his eyes traveled to her lips.

Lexi jerked back as though she'd been stung and shook her head. "I can't do this, Lance."

He dropped his arms. "Lex, I'm…"

She held a hand up to stop him. "I'm drained. I'm going to get inside."

Before she turned away from him, he could see the moisture in her eyes. As the door closed between them, he fought the urge to bang his head against it.

~

Lexi forced her eyes open. It took a few moments for her to realize she'd fallen asleep on the couch. Her legs ached from spending the night curled up in a ball. The dry throb behind her eyes reminded Lexi of the tears that had spilled after coming inside and collapsing. She must have cried herself to sleep.

A quick check of the clock told her it was after nine the next morning. Saturday. Her eyes traveled to the bamboo plant sitting on her kitchen counter. Which made her think about the man who'd given her such a thoughtful gift. Nope, she wasn't going there right now.

She sat up and her stomach churned.

Side effects from the chemo. Fantastic.

Maybe if she ate, her stomach would feel better. Even though eating anything right then was about the last thing she wanted to do.

Her mind went, unbidden, to the night before and the feel of Lance's arms around her. He'd been about to kiss her.

How had things gotten so messed up?

The worst part? She'd wanted him to.

But he deserved better. He deserved someone who could be his partner in life — who could give him a family.

That wasn't her. It could never be her.

Before she started to cry again, she forced herself to get a glass of juice and toast. Even feeling as bad as she did, Lexi recognized that she was being overly emotional and she needed to gain some semblance of control.

Lexi had planned on going to the health food store to pick up supplements to help with the side effects of chemo after her appointment. Because of the unexpected treatment session, she hadn't gotten the chance. As her stomach rolled, she wished she'd taken the time to do it anyway.

The battery indicator on her cell phone was blinking red so she plugged it into the wall. She already dreaded the calls she knew would be coming from concerned family members who needed to make sure she was doing okay. She'd texted them all during the chemo session and then again after she'd gotten home. Since she'd been so exhausted, they'd all promised to wait and call the next day.

Now she wished she'd made the time to talk to them the night before instead.

She sat her empty glass in the sink as her phone

announced a text. She knew who it was even before she checked.

Lance.

"How are you this morning?"

"Nausea. Could be worse."

"I hope you feel better soon. :-(Though I was referring to what happened last night."

She took a deep breath. How was she supposed to respond to that? Another text came through.

"I'm sorry, Lex."

He was apologetic. For trying to kiss her? Or because she'd reacted like an emotional train wreck and had gotten upset?

She was sorry, too, for a number of things.

Lexi's stomach cramped up. With little notice, she ran to the restroom. Everything she'd eaten came back up with a vengeance. She could count on one hand the number of times she'd vomited in her life. Grams claimed she had an iron stomach

It would seem it'd met its match in the chemotherapy.

Sitting on the cool floor in the bathroom, she hugged her knees to her chest and willed the pain and nausea to end.

Unable to think much past the moment, she texted back, "Sick right now. Will write more later."

Chapter Nine

After spending all day in the workshop, Lance was happy to end his Saturday. He'd had plenty of work to do to keep him busy plus he'd gotten caught up after taking Friday off. It still hadn't been demanding enough to stop worrying about Lexi. He'd gone back and forth between imagining her resting the day away and being on the verge of driving by her place to make sure she was okay.

She never did text back after saying she was sick. The truth was, he wouldn't have blamed her if she'd said she was sick so she could avoid talking to him.

His shoulders rose as he sighed.

Lance never should have tried to kiss her. How could he have been that stupid? He didn't doubt his own feelings. But he was sure she still saw him as her little brother's best friend.

By the time he'd eaten dinner, he was getting

concerned. What if she needed help or was truly sick? Unwilling to let his imagination get the best of him, he caved in and called Tuck.

"Hey, man. What's up?"

Lance smiled at the sound of his friend's voice.

"How are you guys doing?"

"We're good. Laurie made fried chicken. You'll hear no complaints here."

"I bet not!" He paused. "Have you heard from Lexi today? I got a text from her earlier saying she was sick and hadn't heard from her since."

"I spoke with her after lunch and mom called her this afternoon. She's feeling better. She was having a lot of nausea and vomiting this morning but by lunch, it had faded. I think she was planning on sleeping this afternoon."

"Oh good. I'm glad. Here's hoping that'll be the worst of it for her after this first session."

"No kidding. Lance, I'm sure you could call her and check in. She wouldn't mind."

Lance said nothing. Tuck didn't miss a beat.

"Uh oh. What did you do?"

"I'm not going there today, Tuck."

Which was undoubtedly the wrong thing to say to his friend. The guy never turned his back on a challenge. "Do I need to drive by and check on my sister?" His tone was serious.

"I screwed up. But it won't happen again. Besides, she may never speak to me and it'll all be a non-issue anyway."

"Okay, spill it or I'll go over and get the story from her."

Tuck had always been protective of his sisters. Lance got it, he felt the same way about his own.

With a sigh, Lance told his best friend about his feelings and how he'd tried to kiss her last night. His neck was warm by the time he'd finished.

Tuck chuckled. "It's about time, man. She'll come around."

"You don't want to come over and bash me for making your sister upset?"

"A more romantic situation might have been better. But it doesn't take much to make her mad. Truthfully, I've been pulling for the two of you for years."

The heat in Lance's neck intensified along with his disbelief. That he had Tuck's blessing for how he felt was a good thing. But he still had to get Lexi to talk to him again. Which, knowing the woman, might not be so easy.

"Lance?"

"Yeah?"

"The longer you wait, the worse it'll be."

"The pressure helps. Thank you."

"Anytime." Tuck laughed and hung up the phone.

Lance wracked his brain for a way to show Lexi that he was sorry. He wanted her to know he cared, but knew he needed to back way off. At least for now.

~

There was a knock at the door and Lexi groaned. She'd already been on the phone with Tuck, her mom, Grams, and even Serenity for a few moments. After being sick earlier in the day, muscles she never knew she had ached. At least she was no longer sprawled out on the bathroom floor. That was an improvement. If she had a half day like that after each chemo session, she should consider herself lucky.

Still, the last thing she wanted to deal with was a visitor.

Trying to place a pleasant expression on her face, she opened the door. As soon as she saw Lance, she sighed.

"Before you slam the door in my face, I come bearing gifts. And a huge apology."

The way his blue eyes implored her wore down her resolve. Or maybe she was way too drained to put up a fight. She stepped aside and motioned for him to enter.

He walked in and placed a large bag on the table. She watched as he withdrew several cartons and even took out a small vase complete with a purple rose.

Lance did it all with a single-minded focus.

After he retrieved a bowl and spoon from her kitchen, he placed those on the table next to the cartons.

"I've got chicken noodle soup from Daisy Belle's Diner. I brought you a bottle of ice-cold tea and lots of saltines. Crackers always seemed to help me when my stomach was giving me trouble."

It was only after he'd arranged everything just so that he turned to face her.

His thoughtfulness — combined with that open and hopeful look on his face — warmed Lexi's heart. She felt herself relax as a smile fought its way out.

"You didn't have to do this. Thank you."

"You were on my mind all day and I wanted to do something to help you feel better. And I'm sorry about yesterday. I…" He stopped and she could tell he was searching for the right words.

"Lance, I know I overreacted. I felt overwhelmed already and you threw me for a loop. Maybe I misunderstood the whole thing."

"I hate for you to be upset with me. It's the last thing I want."

Did the fact that he glossed right over her last comment mean she hadn't misunderstood his intentions at all? She tried to glean more specifics from his expression but came away empty handed.

"It's hard to be upset with a guy who drives me to Dallas — twice. And brings me food. Not to mention who puts up with my bad moods."

The relief on his face made her smile.

"Good. I'm glad." He peered over his shoulder at the door. "I'll let you rest. Are you going to church tomorrow?"

"Not this week. The way I'm feeling today, I have a hard time imagining I'll be up to it in the morning."

"If you need anything, don't hesitate to call."

"Thank you."

She watched him leave.

There was no doubt about it — the man went out of his way to help those in his life. She respected him for that.

Even as kids he'd been nice. Sure, Lance and Tuck had gotten on her nerves. Often. But he'd always been kind to both Lexi and Serenity. When he brought snacks or treats to their house, he had enough to split between the four of them. Lance had been like another brother.

That certainly wasn't the case anymore.

If it hadn't been for her surgery…

No, she wouldn't go there.

What was the point now?

Sadness descended on Lexi and she sank back down on the futon.

Good guys were hard to find and she'd had one under her nose most of her life.

~

Lance dove into his breakfast as Tuck filled him in on the renovations he and Laurie were planning on doing over the coming months.

"It'll be good to open up that second bathroom. It's cramped and the coloring is terrible. I tolerated it because I saw it once a month when I went in and cleaned it."

"I was in there once and you're right — anything you can do will only help."

Tuck studied him over the rim of his glass of milk. "Lexi seemed herself last night at dinner. You guys okay?"

"We're fine. The fence of friendship is now mended."

Tuck was instantly alert at the choice of words. "Is that not what you were hoping for?"

Lance didn't want to discuss it right now. Not here in the middle of a restaurant, anyway. "We aren't arguing and she doesn't hate me. I'll take it."

"What happened?"

"I'm her little brother's best friend."

Tuck appeared doubtful but had the good sense to not say anything else about it.

Lexi hadn't texted Lance at all the last two days. After texting back and forth several times a day for the last couple of weeks, he missed the contact. It confirmed what he had feared: she only thought of him as a friend and he may have messed that up, too.

The rest of his Monday flew by. He had an unusually large number of customers walk into the shop with custom jobs he added to his schedule. It surprised him how satisfying it was to have people seek him out after seeing his work. He knew his dad would be proud.

Lance put his tools away, dusted his hands off, and reached for his cell phone. There were three texts.

Two were from his sisters. One was from Lexi.

The moment he saw her name, his pulse skittered. He tapped on his phone to bring up the message.

"Thanks again for the soup. How has your day been?"

It was crazy how words on a screen had the power to take his spirits and make them soar.

Smiling, he typed back, "You're welcome. It's been crazy busy. How are you doing?"

"Better. Friday and Saturday were not shining moments in my past. I'll keep it in mind after my next session and insist on maintaining hermit status."

":-(I'm glad you're better though. When do you go back to work?"

"A week from today and I'm more than ready. It'll be weird after being off for this long."

Lance imagined it would. He already planned on coming by for lunch one day. Or maybe he should text her first and make sure she didn't mind.

"You'll be okay. I'll bet the hospital's had a hard time functioning without you."

"I appreciate that. I hope you have a relaxing evening."

"Thanks. You, too."

And that was the last of the texts he received. By

the time he left the workshop, he was whistling, his mood lighter than it had been in days.

~

"How's Lexi doing?"

The question came from Vera Davenport. Lance had told his parents how much he'd been helping Lexi the last month. Even though he'd had to take a few extra days off to take her to Dallas, he'd kept up with the work at the shop.

"She's good. She was sick Saturday but is feeling okay now. She's handling the whole thing like a pro."

"I remember her. She always seemed mature for her age." Vera moved a plate of cookies over on the coffee table so they were closer to her son. Peter reached to grab one for himself, too.

Lance was still getting used to seeing him with that crooked smile — one of the many reminders the stroke left behind. The strength in those muscles had improved with therapy, but the one side of his face was visibly more relaxed than the other. A fact that held true for that entire half of his body.

The stroke had changed the man sitting in front of Lance and it saddened him. The whole family knew they needed to accept this new normal, even if it wasn't what any of them would have wanted for Peter.

Still, he knew his dad was lucky to be alive. And they were blessed that the stroke occurred in the right hemisphere of the brain because it meant there was no damage to Peter's ability to speak. It also spared his dominant hand.

"Are you serious about her?"

"Excuse me?" Lance gawked at Vera. That question had come out of nowhere. What was it with people? Apparently he'd become an open book of emotions since he left the force.

She threw him an innocent look across the rim of her glass of sweet iced tea. "I know you, Lance."

She did. And both parents had been privy to his infatuation with Lexi when they were kids, too. He thought about the last few weeks and realized he'd given them a lot of updates about her. Admittedly more than he might have given if he were talking about a friend.

"Yes, I'm serious about her."

Peter gave him a satisfied nod.

Lance popped the last bite of cookie in his mouth, dusted his hands off, and swallowed. "Can we change the subject now?"

Vera smiled. "What was it you wanted to talk about?"

"I've been thinking about family a lot and how things can change in the blink of an eye." He wasn't referring to just Lexi and it was clear they knew it. "Our family has gotten so spread out and I thought maybe we should try and change that. At least once a year, anyway."

"What do you have in mind, son?" The question came from Peter, which encouraged Lance.

"We used to go to the renaissance festival every year as a family. It's been a long time since we've done that. Now, it's too late to go to the one in Oklahoma. But I checked and the huge one down in Houston is going on now through November. I think we should try to get as many of us to go together in the next couple of weeks as we can and then make the festival in Oklahoma a new tradition." He sat back and tried to gauge their reactions.

Peter and Vera exchanged a look.

"We were just talking the other day about how we missed having everyone together more," Vera said. "But I don't know that many of your sisters would be interested."

"I've already called them all to see. Marian's family can't be there for obvious reasons. Avalon won't be able to make it but said she's excited about starting the tradition next year and promised to meet us in Oklahoma. Gwen and Liz were all for it." He was getting excited about the idea and the hope on both of his parents' faces right now told him they were, too. "Come on, what do you guys say?"

Peter clapped his hands together. "I say we go for it. It'll be fun!"

"I agree." Vera nodded, reaching over for a pad of paper and a pen she kept on a table nearby. "I wish Marian could come but I wouldn't want to walk around a festival that pregnant, either." She chuckled. "But next year, I hope we can all go together. Make it a family reunion of sorts."

Lance was smiling but he cleared his throat. "Do you mind if I invite Lexi to go with us?"

Peter gave him a wink. "I think you should."

Vera gave a swift nod. "Besides, maybe by next year, she will be family." She raised an eyebrow at him.

The back of his neck got warm as he shook his head. "Don't get too ahead of yourself there, Mom."

She laughed and got up to hug him. "No pressure, Lance."

"I mentioned it to her the other day. I hadn't

talked to you guys yet, so we didn't discuss it further. I think this would be good for her."

While Vera made a list of things to do before the fair, Lance's thoughts went to Lexi. He hoped she'd agree to go with him. He should probably give her a heads up about his family, though. When his sisters brought a man home to a family gathering, their parents didn't take it lightly. In fact, they assumed the relationship was getting serious if it got to that point. He doubted their reaction to Lexi would be any different.

~

It was Wednesday evening and a knock at the door startled Lexi. She checked the peephole to find Tuck standing on the other side.

She opened the door. "Don't you have a wife to go home to?"

"Yes, as a matter of fact, I do. She's beautiful, sweet, talented, makes me smile, and she's got chicken enchiladas in the slow cooker. This is a happy man who's looking forward to getting home."

Lexi laughed. "Steady there, Prince Charming. With life so good back at the castle, what brings you here to talk with the commoners?" She winked at him.

He gave her an appreciative grin and a hug. "I have three things I want to talk to you about."

Lexi motioned to the futon and joined him. His tone was serious and she waited for him to begin.

"Mom mentioned that Serenity has wanted to talk to you. We all know the two of you haven't gotten along in years. There's a lot that has gone unsaid.

Mom got the impression Serenity would like to bury some of it."

"Okay." Tuck couldn't have surprised her more. What was she supposed to do about Serenity? She'd been the one who'd tried to put the past behind them, only to wind up beating her head against a brick wall. It had happened often enough, and she no longer felt the pain from the impacts.

"If Serenity calls and wants to meet for lunch or something, please don't turn her down."

Lexi jerked and ignored the protest from her healing muscles. "I've never turned her away. I've tried to get through to her for years. If she makes the first move and wants to get together to talk about things, I won't tell her no. But I won't initiate it. Not this time."

He held both hands up in surrender. "I totally get it and I don't blame you. I wanted to give you a head's up in case she calls you. Maybe recent events have reminded her what's important in life."

"It's possible. Or it's just talk. I hope you're right, though." She'd wanted to repair her relationship with Serenity for so long and it was difficult to imagine making any progress in that area. Ready to talk about something else, she nudged the conversation along. "That's one reason."

"Laurie wanted me to extend an invitation. She's done a lot of research on chemo treatments and knows that, while it doesn't always happen, some people lose their hair." He paused. "If you're interested, she said she would be happy to take portraits of you now in case that happens. Then you can have before and after pictures if that's something you're interested in."

Lexi knew that she might lose her hair. It wasn't something that happened right away and she had pushed it back into the recesses of her mind. "Tell her I appreciate the thoughtful offer and will take her up on that."

"Good. Do you want to come over for dinner tomorrow? Laurie could take the pictures at our house, that way you can be comfortable and stay off your feet. I'll even come by and pick you up."

"That works for me." She was more than ready to get out of her apartment for a while — it'd been getting smaller by the day. They settled on a time for him to come by and get her. "And the other thing? You usually leave the whopper for last."

Tuck chortled. "You know me well. I want to talk about Lance."

She knew he was judging her initial reaction and had no idea how she'd fared. "What about him?" The friends had always talked and there was no doubt in her mind that Lance had told her brother about the almost kiss.

"He was worried that you would be upset with him after Friday night. I wanted to see if you guys were okay."

"We're fine, Tuck. He brought me food Saturday evening. We texted a few times this week. We've forgotten the whole thing."

"I doubt that."

All she'd wanted was to avoid this line of questioning, but it didn't look like that was going to happen tonight. She shot him a warning glare, one that rolled right off his back. "Spit it out."

"Lance is a great guy. You've always gotten along well. Do you still see him as just a friend?"

"I don't think this is any of your business, Kentucky Chandler." There was a look of triumph on Tuck's face and she groaned. "It doesn't matter one bit what I think or how I see him. We stay friends because there's going to be someone out there who's better for him than I am."

"That's not true."

"It is. He should find a woman who can give him a family."

It took a moment for the meaning of her words to sink in, and then Tuck reached over and pulled her to his side. "Lexi, there's more to a relationship and marriage than a biological child. I can tell you right now that if Laurie found out she could never get pregnant, I would love her the same."

"This is different."

"Maybe. But it's not like Lance doesn't know the situation. You're not even willing to give him a chance?"

She shook her head. What chance was it? He deserved better and she wasn't going to open that door to have it slammed shut in her face when Lance finally realized that.

"I like Lance. I value our friendship and I hope he's okay with that." A thought hit her and she scooted away from Tuck enough to face him. "Are you going to report all of this back to him?"

"You know if you asked me to not say anything, I wouldn't."

"I know. Maybe if you tell him what I told you, he'll get where I'm coming from. I don't want to hurt him and I don't want to lose him as a friend."

"And what about you? How do you feel about the whole thing?"

She shrugged but refused to answer because she wasn't sure herself. All she knew was that both of them could be hurt way too easily if things ever went forward from where they were now.

"Really? That's it?"

"Yep."

Tuck pulled her into a hug again. "You are selling yourself way too short." When he leaned back to study her face, he asked her, "Do you have anyone lined up to take you to your next chemo session?"

"No. I planned on driving myself. But on the off chance I react worse this time than last, I better not."

"Say the word and I'll put in for the time off that day."

"Can I let you know Friday? Is a week enough time?"

"That'll be fine." He gave her shoulders another squeeze and stood. "I've got to go. Sleep well tonight and I'll see you on Sunday."

Lexi saw him to the door. With all the thoughts swirling around in her head, sleep wasn't likely to come anytime soon.

Chapter Ten

L ance began work on a set of cabinets that he would eventually install in a customer's bathroom. His mind replayed the conversation he and Tuck had over the phone earlier in the day.

When his friend had told him what Lexi said, it had stunned Lance to no small degree. Once he'd realized he'd fallen in love with Lexi, his mind had gone over many different reasons why Lexi might never feel the same way.

That she was unable to have children had never entered the equation.

Sure, he'd thought about having a family someday. More and more, he was feeling that family just might be Lexi. He couldn't imagine his life without her now. When it came to having kids, they could adopt. He and Tuck had known a guy at the force a few years ago who adopted an infant from China when he and his wife were unable to have kids of their own. There were children in the foster care system right here in Texas who needed parents.

He wished he knew if Lexi's misgivings originated from trying to protect him, or if it was because of how she felt about herself. He suspected it was a combination of both.

Tuck had specifically said that she never conceded she didn't have feelings for him. She was afraid their friendship would be ruined. Lance respected that and it gave him as much hope as anything could have right now.

How could he convince Lexi he thought she was whole and perfect for him the way she was?

He'd made it to mid-afternoon when a voice spoke from the doorway. The subject of his thoughts was standing there, her arms crossed, doubt shadowing her pretty face.

"It's good to see you, Lex." Lance's mouth went dry and he cleared his throat. He motioned to the chair in the corner and dragged another over near it. When she'd had a seat, he joined her. "You look like you're feeling a lot better today." She moved freely and didn't seem to be in any pain.

"Much. I'm supposed to relax the rest of this week, but I've got to get out of my house before I'm having conversations with the bamboo plant. I'm an hour away from naming it."

Lance laughed. "That's definitely not a good sign." He studied her, waiting for her to speak and give him a reason for her visit.

She glanced around the room as though she was searching for something. "It's here, isn't it?"

He raised an eyebrow at her, quickly scanning the area himself. "What?"

"The elephant."

Getting her meaning, he chuckled. "I call him

Goober."

Her eyes shone as she smiled at him. "Very appropriate." She shrugged. "I'm tired of it hanging around. I'm sure Tuck talked to you. He always talks to you."

Lance knew his expression must have confirmed her suspicions. He watched a shade of pink dust her cheeks as she ran her fingers through her hair.

He reached a hand up to scratch the back of his neck. "I don't know what to say."

She squared her shoulders and met his eyes with confidence. "That you don't think less of me. That we're still friends."

"I could never think less of you. You're one of the bravest women I've ever known." A shadow of doubt passed over her eyes. He wished he could erase it from her mind completely. "We'll always be friends. No matter what else happens between us. There are too many years of history for that to change."

Lexi visibly relaxed against the back of her chair. "I'm glad."

Lance meant every word he'd just said. But he wasn't going to leave it at that. "For the record, I respect what you told Tuck. But I officially disagree."

"With what?"

"Lex, I have a difficult time believing there's anyone out there better for me than you are. Just as you are."

She fidgeted with the hem of her shirt but maintained their eye contact. "In the spirit of friendship, how about we drop this line of conversation?"

"Agreed." He gave her a winning smile. "And in the spirit of friendship, how about you grant me permission to escort you to Dallas next week?"

She was shaking her head. "I don't think that's a good idea."

"Why?" Lance did everything he could to keep the humor he felt from showing on his face.

He watched Lexi struggle as she weighed her options. If she really felt they were just friends, she shouldn't hesitate to take him up on his offer.

The very fact that she was wavering gave Lance hope that she felt more, even if she wasn't ready to consider the possibility.

Lexi flashed him a frown. Her lips were pressed together so hard that they'd turned white. She clenched her jaw and exhaled slowly before muttering, "Fine."

"Good. That's settled."

She glared at him. "So we're clear, I know exactly what you did there." She lifted her chin and left the workshop.

Lance laughed. He moved so he could see out the window.

The dark-haired beauty marching away from his workshop was one of the most stubborn women he'd ever met.

~

When Lexi stepped into Tuck and Laurie's house, Rogue ran up to greet her. The black and white border collie's tail was wagging with such exuberance, his entire rear end was moving back and forth.

"No jumping, boy." Tuck put a hand out in front of Rogue.

Lexi didn't remember Rogue ever jumping, but the

thoughtfulness of her brother warmed her heart. She patted the dog's head and then laughed when he ran off and returned with a tennis ball.

"I'm not sure I've seen him without one in his mouth for long."

Laurie peeked her head around the corner from the kitchen. "It's like his pacifier."

Lexi laughed. "I believe that."

Chelsea Blake, Laurie's younger sister, came into the room and waved. "How are you, Lexi?"

"I'm good, thanks! How about you? Are you used to the small town life yet?"

Chelsea had gone to a big college and then moved to New York to work for a law firm. The sisters' relationship was precarious at best. After Laurie had been stabbed, Chelsea decided it was time to change that. She moved to Kitner to help Laurie recover. After Tuck and Laurie got married, Chelsea moved into the small apartment above the photography studio.

Chelsea had been helping out at the studio and holding several part-time jobs. She liked to tell everyone she was giving herself through the end of the year to decide what she was doing for the rest of her life. After following what her parents had wanted her to do, she figured she owed herself that much.

Lexi didn't blame her.

"I'm loving Kitner." Chelsea flopped onto a recliner. "The longer I'm here, the more I realize how unhappy I was in New York."

"I'll be right out!" Laurie's voice floated from the kitchen.

"No need to hurry. Do you need any help in there?" Lexi called back.

"I've got everything under control. Make yourself comfortable."

Lexi sat on the couch and accepted the tennis ball from Rogue. She threw it into the hallway and the dog tore off after it.

Tuck patted her shoulder. "I'll go see if I can help her. I think she wanted to do the photo session first then we'll have dinner."

"Sounds like a plan."

Lexi liked the way Tuck's house felt now that he and Laurie were married. She brought her own sense of style into the home. Goodness knows the place needed it.

There was a large, framed picture of Rogue on one wall. He was laying down, gazing at something off to the side. It was the kind of picture that could have been included in a dog breeding magazine. Laurie had taken it back before she and Tuck were officially a couple and later gave it to him for his birthday.

"They sure are happy together," Lexi commented to Chelsea.

"Yeah, it's almost sickening at times." She chuckled. "I'm glad for them, though. This is the first time in years I've had family around. I like it."

Lexi couldn't imagine not being surrounded by her own family.

Laurie came into the room followed by Tuck. She wiped her hands off on a towel and set it down. "Sorry about that! I wanted to get a chocolate cake in the oven quick, giving it time to bake while we're doing photos. Dinner's in the slow cooker and ready when we are."

Chelsea sat up straighter in the chair. "What are we having?"

"Chicken breasts with broccoli and rice topped with cheese."

Laurie smiled with satisfaction at the expressions of appreciation around the room.

"This beautiful woman guarantees I'll never go hungry." Tuck took his wife in his arms and twirled around once, ending with a kiss.

Chelsea caught Lexi's eye and mouthed, "Told you."

Lexi had to fight to keep her laughter at bay.

Laurie did a fantastic job of putting Lexi at ease for the portraits and before long, they were devouring the meal she'd made. It was a perfect evening and the kind of distraction Lexi had desperately needed.

~

It was Friday night and Lexi ran through a mental list of things she needed to get done. Monday she would go back to work at the hospital. She wasn't sure she was ready, although not sitting around her apartment for days on end would be welcome. Her job was a demanding one and she was often on her feet for hours at a time. She didn't look forward to that and anticipated a day or two of sore muscles by the end of her shift.

Most of her coworkers knew she had taken off for a major surgery. But when she'd had to call and tell the head nurse she'd need more time to recover before she could go back, she'd had to tell her why. She hoped the hospital had been discreet about it all. She didn't want people to treat her any differently.

The thought of it caused anxiety to well up in her chest.

"God, I can't control this. If having cancer has taught me anything, it's shown me that. Give me the strength to make it through all of this with the most dignity possible."

She could feel the anxiety settle and she shifted in bed, willing her mind to be quiet and allow her to fall asleep.

Reaching a hand up to rub her forehead, she ran her fingers through her hair absently. Something snagged her attention and she sat up quickly, turning on the light next to the bed.

The image of dark hair lying loose in her hand swam in front of her as her eyes filled with tears. She stared at her pillowcase and the additional strands strewn across its surface.

With a sigh of resignation, she tried to sweep them all into her hand before standing and heading for the trash can in the bathroom. As she passed the mirror, she caught a glimpse of herself.

What would she look like when her hair had all fallen out? She resisted the urge to dig out a baby picture to see the shape of her own skull.

Yeah, sleep wasn't happening.

Lexi's mind raced as she came up with a plan. Tomorrow, she would try to locate brightly-colored surgical caps. She wore them on occasion when she helped out during a surgery at the hospital, but didn't wear them in general. Now, with her hair falling out, she wasn't about to risk having any land on a patient and she surely didn't want a balding spot to become visible.

Yes, covering her head with something would make her feel more secure.

She would go to work wearing a surgical cap and

make that part of her new appearance. Besides, wearing something that was bright and colorful to make the younger patients smile was a good side effect.

It was too bad that wouldn't work for Sunday night dinners.

She could get away with no one noticing this week, but next week would be a different ball game.

~

"It's good to have you back, Chandler."

Lexi returned the smile and waved at Ramirez. She'd already made the second pot of coffee for the day which had earned her the title of hero.

By the middle of her shift, she'd been so tired, she'd attempted to drink a cup of the stuff herself. Three sips into it, she poured the coffee down the sink and tossed the paper cup into the trash.

Nope, that wasn't going to happen.

"We've missed you around here."

Lexi whirled to find Finnegan standing right behind her. She reached up to touch the black and white striped surgical hat she was wearing. "I appreciate that. And you shouldn't sneak up on a person like that. You'll get yourself clobbered."

"Come to dinner with me tomorrow and you can clobber me all you want to." He said it in jest, but his eyes told her otherwise.

"Finnegan. I'm not interested."

"Can't blame a guy for trying."

"And trying. And trying."

He chuckled as he turned to leave. Lexi wished he'd take her seriously and quit asking her out.

The good news was, other than coworkers asking if she was feeling better and telling her they'd missed her, no one had mentioned cancer. To say she was relieved would be an understatement. Kate wasn't on shift or Lexi would thank her for her discretion.

By the time her twelve-hour shift was over, Lexi's abdominal muscles were killing her. She wasn't sure she'd ever been that tired. It was all she could do to drag herself home and in bed.

When her day off finally arrived, she slept all day and it wasn't until early Saturday that she woke up feeling better.

It was almost ten in the morning when there was a knock at the door. Lexi frowned at the gym shorts and oversized t-shirt she was wearing. Taking a glance through the peephole in the door, she saw Serenity standing outside. She snatched a handkerchief off the counter and swept her rapidly thinning hair back and secured it over her head before opening the door.

Serenity hesitated. "I hope I didn't wake you up."

"Not at all." Lexi stood to the side and ushered her younger sister in. "Where's Gideon?"

"He's with Mom and Grams. They're watching a movie this morning."

"That sounds like fun. How's everything been going for you guys?" Lexi sat down and Serenity joined her.

"It's fine." Serenity's long hair flowed down and touched the seat of the couch. "His therapists have been happy with his progress. I think we may get a new speech therapist, though. That should be a lot of fun."

There was no missing the sarcasm in Serenity's voice. Lexi knew that consistency was better for

Gideon. Change, especially with regards to something as important as a therapist, wasn't easy on him.

"I'm sorry. I'll be praying that, if he does, the transition will go smoothly."

"Thanks." Serenity shifted her position. "How was your first week back at work?"

"It nearly killed me." Lexi rubbed her eyes and knew there were dark circles beneath them. "I'm kidding. Mostly. I'm sure next week will be easier."

"I'm sure it will. How are you feeling?"

"I feel tired a lot, but otherwise I'm fine. It took longer than I wanted it to for the incisions to heal."

Serenity nodded. "I imagine." Her eyes went to the kerchief on her head. "And the new fashion statement?"

Lexi knew that the question was coming. She knew she would have to share with family about her hair falling out. She hadn't expected to tell Serenity first. But her little sister was trying to make an effort — which was more than she had done in years. Lexi took a deep breath and removed the kerchief.

Serenity took in the thinning hair and few bald patches. The sympathy in her eyes was almost too much for Lexi. It was rapidly replaced with humor and Lexi didn't know if she should expect to laugh or kick her sister out of the apartment. "What?"

"I'm sorry. I'm picturing you in wild looking wigs right now." A giggle escaped.

Lexi tried to glare at her but failed and the two erupted in a laughter that did a lot of good for her spirit.

Lexi wiped a tear from her eye as she tried to get her giggles under control. "I don't think I'm going to mess with wigs. I'm kind of getting used to the handkerchiefs. Besides, I needed to tell my coworkers sooner than later anyway."

"I think the handkerchiefs are just fine." Serenity reached over and fingered a section of her sister's locks. "I've always loved your hair."

The comment shocked Lexi. "Really? I've always loved yours."

The sisters laughed again.

Lexi shrugged. "I've heard women can experience hair changes when it grows back after chemo. Who knows, maybe I'll be a curly blonde a year from now."

They giggled until both were leaning against the futon in exhaustion.

When Serenity spoke, her face was serious. "Here's the thing, Lexi. I hate I haven't been there for you lately. I'm sorry I haven't offered to take you to a chemo session."

Lexi shook her head. "Don't think another thing about it. I've got help and I'm okay. Gideon is your priority and that's how it should be. No need to stress him out any more than necessary — or yourself."

"I'm sorry for the last five years, too."

The words wrapped themselves around Lexi's heart. Tears sprang to her eyes and she desperately tried to keep them at bay. Only now did she register how much pain she had experienced when her only sister had been angry with her. "Thanks, Serenity. I've missed you, do you know that?"

"I've missed you, too."

Lexi wanted to hug her sister but wasn't sure if Serenity was open to it. She knew little about her sister as a grown woman and a mother. She couldn't recall the last time they had sat around and chatted like this. She hoped this would be the first of many opportunities to reconnect with her.

Serenity cleared her throat. "You know, you should keep a section of your hair in a baggy. That way, when it grows back, you can compare it and see if it did change shades."

"That's a good idea." Lexi moved to put the handkerchief back on her head but Serenity stopped her.

"I still love your hair."

Lexi reached for her sister then, giving her a hug that was long overdue.

~

Lexi strode into the cafeteria, her mind on one thing. Food.

It was because of this single-minded focus she didn't notice Finnegan until he stepped into her path. Her foot collided with his shoe and she sighed. When he didn't keep walking, she bit back a comment.

"You've been like a woman on a mission the last couple of days. It's been hard to catch you."

"I'm trying to get back into the swing of things at work."

"I saw the schedule and you're off Friday. How about joining me for a movie and dinner?"

The exhaustion of the day coupled with the fact that the man was keeping her from her tacos caused an immediate reaction. "I can't. I have chemotherapy that day. How does Sunday work for you?"

Finnegan's mouth opened in surprise. "You have cancer?"

"Yes. Ovarian. I was off for several weeks recovering from a complete hysterectomy and now

I'm going through chemo treatments." She hadn't talked about any of it at work and now it felt somewhat relieving to blurt it out.

"Wow. I didn't realize that."

"Finnegan. It's okay. I'm fine." She paused. "How about Sunday?" She already knew what he would say.

"I think I'm tied up that day. I'll get back to you sometime next week."

"That'll work."

Finnegan said his goodbye and disappeared.

It wasn't anything more than she had expected. But the fact was, when he'd heard about her illness, he hadn't wasted any time going elsewhere.

She had no interest in the man whatsoever. His reaction did, however, confirm her suspicions. Most men her age wouldn't want to be with a woman who couldn't give him a family. Not even Finnegan, who seemed to have very few things on his list to avoid when it came to dating women.

The realization was like a shot to the heart.

Chapter Eleven

When Lexi turned after speaking with a doctor, her expression made Lance's stomach tighten and he gritted his teeth. What on earth did the guy say to bring one of the saddest expressions he'd ever seen to her face?

The doctor was lucky he'd headed the other way. Another glimpse at Lexi and he was impressed by how quickly she could compose herself. Her eyes found him and the flash of relief was clear, even across the cafeteria.

Without giving the food a second thought, she headed his way. He stood.

"Are you okay?"

"I don't want to talk about it." Lexi took a seat and stared at the table. There was a blue surgical cap on her head with frogs all over it. She slumped in her chair, dark circles under her eyes.

"I'll go grab us lunch. What's your preference?"

"Three crunchy beef tacos, please."

"You got it."

By the time he got back, Lexi was acting more like herself. He set the plate in front of her and she wasted no time tackling the first taco.

He joined her in his meal, observing her complete focus on anything but him.

"I don't know whether to ask what's wrong or pretend to ignore that you're upset."

His words brought her eyes to his. The pools of dark brown were a storm of emotions. He didn't know which one to focus on.

Lance sighed. "Do I need to go have a talk with that doctor?"

That got a reaction. She set her napkin down and straightened her spine. "Of course not."

He gave her one of his most serious stares until she relented.

"Finnegan is always asking me out." She glanced around her and lowered her voice to just above a whisper. "He asks almost every nurse out. I'm tired of telling him no and may have mentioned that I had cancer and was going through chemo after a complete hysterectomy. I guess that did the trick."

She went back to eating but Lance didn't miss the tremor in her voice.

"He's a jerk who wouldn't know a first class woman if she punched him in the face." He paused. "Which I give you credit for not doing."

Lexi snorted and covered her mouth with a hand as she finished chewing. Once she'd swallowed, she chuckled.

"If I had, it would have been the talk of the ER for weeks. 'Good ole Chandler, she can save a five-year-old and throw a mean right cross, all in the same morning.'"

"Any man who wouldn't want to date a woman like that is insane." He meant every word of that. She was a woman who stood up for herself and he admired that about her. Yep, Finnegan was a complete idiot.

"Thank you." She observed him. "If I ever take your friendship for granted, give me a swift kick to set me straight again."

He raised an eyebrow at her. "I'll remember that."

The music of her laughter kicked Lance's pulse into high gear and his mouth went dry. He tried to focus on his food, but he couldn't take his eyes off the amazing woman sitting across from him.

That any man would see her as lacking in any way was unfathomable to him. Her strength and humor gave her what she needed to get through any challenge — and that included this one she faced now.

He prayed that God would help her see how much she had to offer.

~

Friday started off early. Lexi had mentioned wanting to get to Dallas in the morning so she could go by a particular natural food store for a few things. Lance was happy to oblige.

His eyes went to the handkerchief on her head when she got into the passenger side of his Jeep. She must have caught the glance because a hand flew to her head as she tucked the sides into place.

Unable to help himself, he reached for Lexi's hand and held it in his, moving it away from her head.

"You never have to feel uncomfortable around me, Lex. Ever." The feel of her hand in his had his heart hammering. Despite the intense desire to hold onto her hand for a while longer, Lance squeezed it gently and released it to grasp the steering wheel. He swallowed hard.

She took in a slow breath and settled into her seat.

Lance wished he could have a clue to what she was thinking.

If he had to guess, he'd bet that Lexi was losing her hair. She'd never been one to wear a hat of any kind. He doubted she had gained a desire to wear a handkerchief now.

"Does your family know?"

"Serenity does. Everyone else will figure it out on Sunday night. I'm going to stay home from church. I don't want to announce it to the world there." Her attention was on the landscape outside her window as they headed out of town.

"Serenity knows, huh? Wow, I wouldn't have guessed that. How'd that go down?"

"She came by the other day to visit. She even apologized for the last five years. It was weird. And relieving."

"That's great, Lex! I know that's been rough for a long time now."

"It has." She relaxed into her seat, a serene expression on her face. "I hope it continues like this. I've missed her."

"God sometimes uses situations like yours to build bridges and mend relationships. It sounds like that may be what He's doing here. I'm happy for you two."

"I sure hope so. It's more than I ever expected."

She wrapped a few strands of hair around one finger. "It's going to upset my mom."

"Was it a surprise to you?"

"Losing my hair?"

He nodded.

"Yes and no. I expected it to happen, but when I first noticed it, I wasn't prepared. Seeing big bunches of hair at once was disconcerting. I'm combing through it right before bed and again in the morning to keep it from falling out everywhere."

"That's a good idea." He studied her out of the corner of his eye. He tried to imagine what she would look like without those black tresses framing her face. It was difficult.

"Don't worry, I won't shed all over your car."

When he saw the teasing glint in her eyes, he laughed loudly.

~

Lexi paid for her hand basket full of items. Between the vitamins, tea, and three bottles of essential oils she had read would help with the nausea and vomiting after chemo, it was more than she had expected to buy. If any of it helped, though, it would be worth it.

Lance followed her with two organic oatmeal raisin cookies. When they exited the store, he handed one to her. "We still have a couple of hours before your session begins. What's the plan?"

She felt her face get warm.

"I…I was thinking I might go by a salon and get the rest of my hair shaved off." Now the heat in her cheeks spread to her entire head. She imagined it looked like it was on fire as she focused her attention on removing the plastic surrounding her cookie. "I'm ready for it to be gone."

A hand on her shoulder brought her attention to Lance.

"I don't blame you. Do you have a place in mind?"

Forty minutes later, Lexi was sitting in a chair at a hair salon as the remaining dark strands fell to the floor. She'd already put some in a plastic bag at home, but it still seemed odd to get up and walk away from the last of her hair.

The stylist, whose name was Annie, was very professional. She said just the right things, got it all shaved off, and even applied an oil to help with any irritation and to make her head smooth.

When Lexi saw her reflection in the mirror, the waves of emotions were overwhelming. Relief at not having to worry about her hair shedding battled with the anxiety of what people might think when they saw her. She experienced awe at how smooth and shiny her head was. She laid a hand on the exposed skin.

"This is great. It feels much better. Thank you." She smiled at the kind stylist and turned for her bag. "How much do I owe you?"

The other woman shook her head of brown curls. "Don't you even think about it. Please go with my prayers for a speedy and complete recovery."

Now Lexi's tears blurred Annie's features. "Thank you," she whispered as she accepted a hug. Offering one last smile of appreciation, she tied the handkerchief over her head.

Lance was outside, sitting on a bench under a tree, reading something on his cellphone. When he spotted her, he jumped up, his face a mixture of curiosity and concern. "How'd it go?"

"It's all gone. It was so thin, it didn't take her long, although it seemed like a lot there on the floor."

"And how do you feel?"

"Relieved." When her hair had first fallen out, shaving it all would have made her sad. But now, not having to worry about hair tumbling onto patients or waking up with a pillow full of it was liberating. Funny how perspective changed things. "I feel good."

His eyes traveled to her handkerchief. "I'm glad. Do you want to get something to eat?"

Lexi's stomach rolled at the thought of food now that she was close to her session. "No, thank you. The cookie was enough."

"Okay. Should we head over to the cancer center, then?"

"Yeah, I guess so." She had to get through this session and then she'd only have one more to go. She would make it. And she had to admit that it was comforting to have Lance there with her.

When had she become this dependent on him?

Once her sessions were over, she'd be around him a whole lot less. She didn't like the idea of only seeing him on Sundays at church.

A touch to her elbow claimed her attention. Warmth spread up her arm, her breath catching. She had to stop reacting like that when he touched her.

"Why don't we sit down for a few minutes? We have time."

She nodded her agreement. They took a seat on the bench nearby. "Thanks."

"I don't remember your dad losing his hair when he was dealing with cancer."

"No. Things happened too quickly. He received a

diagnosis and had surgery forty-eight hours later. The surgeon removed what he could, but the cancer had already spread to multiple organs. The recovery from the surgery was a nightmare." Lexi's mind flashed to the dozens of times she'd helped change the dressing on his wounds. They'd been left open to drain. She was trained to do that kind of wound care. It was entirely different, though, when it's your own dad who's groaning in pain. "He went through one radiation and chemotherapy treatment and died a week later."

"I remember being shocked how quickly everything happened. I'm sorry."

"It was hard. The end was horrible and none of us got to say goodbye. There's a lot I wanted to tell him and didn't. But then, I'm not sure another week or a month would have been enough time, either."

"I can't imagine watching someone you love go through that."

She froze as Lance's arm went around her shoulders, his thumb stroking her arm.

They sat like that for a time, listening to the birds chirp in a nearby tree and watching vehicles come and go in the parking lot.

Lexi cleared her throat. "You know, the night after my surgery, I had a dream I'd died like my dad did." His arm tightened around her. "I know it was a combination of the medication and pain that brought it on. I'd forgotten all about it until now."

"You're not going to die, Lex. Not from this."

"I know. Usually I feel confident that it's not my time. Every once in a while, when I'm feeling especially tired, my mind gets carried away. But how can you be that sure?" She turned her body so she could see his face.

The hand on her arm reached up to brush her cheek. "Because you're too stubborn. Plus, I bet your dad's up there right now watching over you and helping you fight this."

His words brought tears to her eyes. She let herself relax, laying her head against his shoulder. Eyes closed, she drew on his strength. He brushed a kiss across the top of her head before leaning his cheek against it.

She sniffed. "You know, I talk to you about things I can't tell anyone else."

"It's all these long car rides we've been going on together. We were going to bond or try to kill each other."

She laughed then, sitting up and swiping away a stray tear. He withdrew his arm, a smile on his face that warmed her heart. "You're an amazing friend, Lance. I'm blessed to have you in my life."

~

Lance felt his heart fill to overflowing. "I feel the same way about you, Alexis Chandler. And before things get any mushier, we'd better go. We wouldn't want to be late for your poison fix."

Her giggles were like music as she stood. "You make it sound so inviting."

As they walked back to his Jeep, he offered her his arm and was pleased when she rested her hand in the crook of his elbow.

At the cancer center, Lance watched as the nurse took a blood sample. She hooked Lexi up to an IV and got the medication flowing. Once that was going, she brought her a cup of water and a blanket in case she got cold.

Twenty minutes later, she'd relaxed with her head leaned back against the chair. A long, quiet sigh combined with her gaze flitting between the clock and the window told him she was restless.

"You look like you're about to jump out of that chair and make a run for it."

"The thought has crossed my mind," she admitted. "I should be thankful I only have to go through three sessions. It could have been worse."

"That it could," he agreed. "But I think you still have the right to hate the experience."

"I appreciate that." She paused. "You know, I was offered a job as a nurse in an oncology department before I graduated."

"I had no idea. I guess you turned it down?"

"I didn't think it was for me. Plus, the job was in Chicago. Now, after all of this, I know oncology would not have been a good fit."

He hadn't realized Lexi moving to Chicago had been an option. Praise God she'd chosen another route. "How did you end up working at the ER?"

"It just kind of happened. I wanted to work in Kitner to be near my family and to help the people in the town I grew up in. I started out on the surgical floor. One day, they needed me to float down to the ER because they were short-handed. The place seemed to fit me like a glove. I got my specialization and moved down there permanently."

Lance shifted to cross his right ankle over the opposite knee. He massaged his chin through his goatee. "At the time? Are you not sure anymore?"

"The hours get to me. But I love being there to

help the kids who come in. That's my favorite part of the job. Doing what I can to make them feel better and get them to smile before they leave again."

He watched as a beam lit up her face.

"Something tells me you're good at your job."

She shrugged. "Well, they haven't fired me yet. I must not be doing too badly." She turned to observe him. "I imagine your parents are proud of how well you're doing at the shop. Tuck mentioned that you've got more business than you have time for."

"It's been busy. But in a good way. Dad's happy with how everything is going, although I think he'd much rather be out there doing the work himself. Sitting around the house is driving him crazy – and my mom, too."

"I imagine. They're lucky they have each other, though."

"That they are."

They were both silent for a while. Lance thought she might have dozed off when she spoke again.

"I meant what I said about being blessed to have you as a friend. Thanks for not giving up on me, even when I'm not the nicest person to be around."

"Trust me, I have my moments, too. For someone going through so much, you're handling it with a lot of grace."

Their eyes locked and Lance could have drowned in the depths of her emotions. He wanted to hold her hand again. Or even better — hold her in his arms.

If she hadn't been tethered to an IV, he would have done just that.

The urge to kiss her was strong. He worked to slow the beating of his heart. Especially when he found her watching him like that, as if she might kiss him back.

Lexi was in a cancer center with medication pumping into her arm. She was tired and vulnerable. This was not the right time.

Now if he could continue to convince himself of that for another couple of hours.

Chapter Twelve

Lexi thought Lance might have tried to kiss her again if they were anywhere else but the center. At the moment, she wasn't sure she would stop him. Which was crazy, right?

She couldn't tear her gaze from his when a nurse walked in with another glass of water. "Are you doing okay, hun?" She set the plastic cup on the table near the bed and picked up the old one.

The interruption was precisely what Lexi needed. The goosebumps on her arms made the hair stand on end and she took a deep breath to steady the galloping of her heart.

"Yes, thank you." A sip of the cold water was another good distraction. By the time the nurse finished checking on her IV and made a few comments, Lexi had pulled her thoughts to a much safer place. After the nurse left, she reached up to make sure her handkerchief was still in place.

"Don't feel like you have to keep wearing it."

She shrugged. The truth was, she would have liked to take it off. But the idea of letting Lance — or anyone — see her bald head for the first time was making her nervous. Maybe that was silly, but she couldn't help it.

"Lance, will you do me a favor?"

"Of course."

"When you talk to Tuck, will you let him know about my hair? Maybe he can prepare my family before Sunday night dinner. I'm not sure I can handle it if my mom falls apart."

"I'll mention it to him tomorrow." He acted like he wanted to say more but stopped himself.

"What is it, Lance?"

He hesitated. "I do talk to Tuck a lot. But I wanted you to know that, from now on, I won't say anything to him about our conversations unless you ask me to. I want you to know you can always trust me."

His words did funny things to her heart and her belly did a flip. She resisted the urge to reach a hand out to him.

"Thank you."

After the chemo session was over, Lance insisted that Lexi get lunch and took her to Cane's again.

"I talked to my parents about the renaissance fair idea and they're excited about it. We're going to go next weekend. Gwen, her husband, and Beth are going to make it, too."

"Oh, that's great! I'm glad they liked the idea!"

He stroked his goatee absently. "I was thinking about something. Why don't you come with us?"

"Me? Why?"

"Because I think you could use a break from everything you're going through. And there's nothing like jumping into the craziness of a renaissance fair to leave that behind and pretend to be someone else."

Lexi could feel her face flush. Spending more time with him appealed to her. But going to the fair with him and his family was a lot different than bumping into him at church or agreeing to have him drive her to Dallas.

On the other hand, he was right. She could use time away from her job, chemo, and everything else that was going on right now.

"Well, goodness knows you've spent plenty of time with my crazy family. It would be fun to go to the fair and get to know yours a little better, too."

His grin was huge. "Great! It's about a five-hour drive there. We need to sit down and go through our schedules. I know my family is planning to drive down on Friday evening, stay in a hotel, go the fair on Saturday, and come back home on Sunday."

"Let me check when I get in to work on Monday. I may have to drive in early Saturday."

"Sounds good. We'll figure it out."

~

Lexi fell asleep for a while on their drive back to Kitner.

By the time he pulled in front of her apartment building, she was feeling relaxed. That chemo session was over and now she could focus on something else for a few weeks.

He walked her to the door of her apartment.

"Thanks again, Lance. I'm hoping these oils and vitamins help. But if it's anything like last time, don't be surprised if I don't text or anything tomorrow."

"I won't worry if you promise me you'll call someone if you get too sick."

"I promise."

"Okay." She thought he would turn and leave. Instead, his gaze traveled to her handkerchief. "Did you keep your head covered because you were uncomfortable?"

She was going to object but gave a small shrug.

"In general? Or with me specifically?"

Lexi thought about that. Mostly in general. Although the more she considered it, the more she realized how nervous she was about what Lance would think.

Which was silly, right?

People would eventually have to see her bare head anyway. Someone was going to be the first and it may as well be him.

Okay, deep breath. Let's get this over with.

She worked to untie the handkerchief at the base of her neck. When she pulled it off her head, the warm breeze hit her skin and it felt amazing.

Lance took in her profile, his gaze traveling from the top of her head to her eyes. Her heart pounded hard in her chest. She was sure he could see it trying to escape like they did in cartoons.

What was he thinking? Was her bald head hammering home she was no longer whole?

He interrupted her thoughts when his hand moved to caress the smooth skin. "In case you have any doubts, you are beautiful."

Tears filled her eyes as his words sunk in. He took a step closer to her and his hand moved to cup the back of her neck. She inhaled sharply. He kissed her then, capturing her lips with such gentleness, she couldn't help but feel treasured.

As she leaned into his kiss, she felt his other arm surround her with strength.

She lost herself in the moment and wasn't sure how much time had passed when their kiss broke.

A sigh escaped at the tenderness on his face. She laid her cheek against his shoulder. "Lance. This isn't a good idea."

"It feels like a good one to me." He kissed her cheek and hugged her close.

Lexi chuckled. "You might feel differently about it tomorrow."

"I doubt that very much. I've wanted to do that since I was sixteen."

She leaned back to study him. "I knew you had a crush on me when we were teens. There's no way that's lasted all this time." He shrugged and she shook her head in amazement.

"What about you? How did you feel when you left for college?"

"I liked you back then, but at eighteen, two years younger is huge. You were Tuck's best friend. I had college."

"It's okay, Lex. You were in another place back then and I understood that. I wondered if you saw me as anything more than Tuck's annoying friend and if you missed me when you left."

"It was very hard for me to go to college. I left all my family. I lost all my friends — and that included you. We practically grew up together. You lived at our house half the time."

Lance laughed, his arms still around her waist. "Tuck saved me from the estrogen overload at my house." He studied her face. "My being two years younger doesn't bother you now?"

"There are a lot of other things I'm more worried about than our age difference."

Like letting herself fall for him when there was a chance he could change his mind. She was still convinced it would happen eventually when he came to his senses.

And she wouldn't think too hard about the consequences if the surgery and chemo didn't work like the doctor thought it would.

It was clear Lance had other questions. Instead of saying anything else, he hugged her again.

"Go get some rest. If you need anything tomorrow, call me."

Lexi swallowed her pride. "Will you bring me another batch of that chicken noodle soup?"

His face lit up. "I'll bring it by at noon. Will that be good?"

"That'll be perfect. Thank you." She smiled up at him, feeling conflicted between wanting him to kiss her again, and needing to escape before he had the chance.

He solved the problem for her when he placed a light kiss to her cheek. "You're welcome. Sleep well and I'll see you tomorrow."

With a small wave, she turned and went inside. She closed the door and leaned against it. She'd wanted to keep her distance — protect her heart. Lexi was pretty sure it was too late for that now.

~

Lance resisted texting Lexi first thing in the morning, hoping she was sleeping in. Instead, he called his oldest sister, Marian. She was always up early with the kids, even on a Saturday.

He updated her on the renaissance fair plans.

"I think it's great Mom and Dad are excited." The sound of two kids laughing made its way through the phone. "I wish we could make it."

"No one expects you to. Are you feeling okay?" He pictured his sister with her blonde hair, short stature, and infectious smile. She was a great mom and he had always looked up to her. She also wore pregnancy well and was one of those women who glowed.

"I'm feeling well. Tired. But then it might be the other kids doing that." She laughed. "I think this is the last one."

"That's what you said after Quinn was born," he reminded her good-naturedly.

"So I did." A child's cry interrupted Marian. "Lance, I've got to go. Speaking of Quinn, he fell and hit his head. Let me know how the fair goes, okay? Love you!"

"I will and I love you, too."

He ended the call, thought for a moment, and dialed Tuck's number.

"Hey, man. What's up?"

"Sorry to call this early. Do you have a few minutes?"

Lance told Tuck about Lexi shaving her head.

"Wow."

"I know. She wanted me to call that way you could give everyone else a heads up before Sunday dinner."

"I appreciate it. I'll talk to them. It'll be good for Mom to process this before she sees Lexi. How's she feeling this morning?"

"I haven't talked to her yet. I'm supposed to take soup by at noon. If you want me to, I can text and let you know. She got some oils and vitamins yesterday, hoping they will help with the nausea and vomiting this time around."

"I hope they work." Tuck spoke to another person in the background. "I've got to run. Thanks for calling and I'll see you on Sunday, huh?"

"Yep, see you then."

Lance kept busy the rest of the morning in the workshop before picking up the soup and heading for Lexi's apartment.

She answered as soon as he knocked. He wondered if she'd been watching for him from the window.

Even though he knew she'd shaved her head and had seen it the day before, it was still the first thing he noticed. He wondered how long that would be the case. He took in her knit shorts and baggy t-shirt. "Hey," was her greeting, along with a welcoming smile.

"Hey yourself." He stepped into the room and she closed the door behind him. All the curtains were drawn and only some of the lights were on. "Is your head bothering you?"

"A little, although it's getting better." She led him into the kitchen. "The oils are helping. Or I suppose it's possible my body wasn't as shocked this time around."

He took the container of chicken noodle soup out of the bag and placed it on the table. "Either way, I'm glad you aren't as sick this time."

She smelled the soup and Lance heard her stomach growl. "Thank you for bringing this."

"Anytime." He wanted to hug her. Or kiss her. He also didn't want to push her, especially if she wasn't feeling well. Instead, he reached for her hand and gave it a gentle squeeze. "Do you need to sit down? I'm only staying for a few minutes."

With a nod, she led them to the futon. She hadn't withdrawn her hand and he was happy to continue holding it in his. He marveled at how delicate it felt in his own as they sat side by side.

"How do the oils work?"

"There are a lot of oils that can help, but I went with frankincense, chamomile, and peppermint. I read that frankincense is supposed to help with healing and that the other two aid in controlling the nausea and vomiting. I've been putting them on my abdomen and on my wrists while the frankincense has been going behind my ears."

He drew her hand closer to him and took a whiff. "It smells good. And it's helping?"

"It's not magic or anything. I still have a lot of nausea. But I haven't had to live in the bathroom today like I did last time."

Her face flushed with the admission and he put a soft kiss to the back of her hand. "I'm relieved, Lex. I know you were miserable, and I doubt you even told us the half of it."

She shrugged and he knew he was right. The woman didn't like asking for help. The fact that she requested the soup was a big step in its own right.

"By the way, I spoke with Tuck and he'll talk to your family before dinner tomorrow night."

"Oh, good. Thank you, Lance."

"Anytime."

They visited a few more minutes before he stood

to leave. He didn't want the food to get cold before she had a chance to eat it. Lance gave her a hug and softly kissed her cheek again on his way out.

He thought about the Chandler family dinner the following night. He hoped it would go well and that Lexi wouldn't be too uncomfortable. While there wasn't anything he could do to help, he wished he could be there for her anyway.

Chapter Thirteen

Lexi checked to be sure her scarf was in place. She'd chosen one that matched the green and brown blouse she was wearing. Now she was standing in front of the Chandler house, trying to work up the courage to go inside.

She reached for the doorknob and gave it a turn. As she stepped into the house, she prayed for strength.

As soon as she had entered the living room, her family turned to look at her. Welcoming smiles, hugs, and laughter made her feel at ease. While Patty's eyes were full of tears, she kept them at bay as she took in Lexi's scarf.

"You know I'm proud of you, Alexis."

"Thanks, Mom."

She heard Grams' voice from the kitchen. "I'll be right there!"

The amusement on Tuck's face made Lexi pause. "What's going on?"

"You'll see." He waggled his eyebrows at her.

When her grandmother entered the living room with a giant smile on her face, Lexi gasped.

Grams had shaved her head — every last silver strand of it. The light from the ceiling fan shone off the pale skin.

The older woman stood in front of her, hands on her hips. "Are you going to leave this old woman hanging? I showed you mine, now you show me yours."

Lexi felt a tickle on her cheek and swiped at it, only now aware of the tears that were flowing. She laughed with a sniff. "Grams, you are something else."

She took her scarf off to rounds of applause. She and Grams posed for several pictures.

Tuck snapped one with his phone. "I'm sending this to Lance," he said, giving her a wink.

Lexi rolled her eyes good-naturedly and went to sit on the couch with Grams. Serenity came to join them, sitting on Lexi's other side.

"It looks good."

"Thanks. It's taken a good ten minutes off my morning routine, too."

Serenity laughed then. "I'll bet it has!" She pulled some of her long hair around. "I have to admit, that's almost tempting."

"Yeah, well, if you shaved your head you'd float away after being used to having such long hair now."

Lexi was busy answering questions about her health. Laurie had been curious about the oils so she was in the middle of showing them to her when Gideon came in from his room. He stopped in front of Lexi, hesitant, his eyes fixed on her head.

"Hi, Gideon! What do you think?" She rubbed her

smooth head with one hand. "It sure looks different, doesn't it?"

His gaze looked at her face and then back at her head.

"Sweetie, you can touch it if you want to. It kind of feels like a bowling ball now."

Lexi wasn't sure what Gideon was thinking. She watched as he reached a hand up to brush the skin. His face was serious and she wanted to think of a way to lighten his mood.

She giggled and pretended to shy away from his hand. "That tickles, Gideon!"

His eyes lit up as he touched her head again, walking his fingers across the top.

She responded with more giggles. "That tickles!" She reached for him and pulled him into her lap, running her fingers across his head. Before long, he was belly laughing and had Lexi joining him.

They played their new game a few more times before Gideon ran back down the hall to his room.

"He's a great kid, Serenity."

Her little sister beamed at her.

Patty came in from the kitchen. "All right, everyone. It's time to eat!"

After dinner, Lexi helped Patty clean up the kitchen before going into the living room and sitting down for a while. Laurie joined her.

"If you want to come by the studio, I would love to take another set of portraits for you." She nodded at Lexi's head. "It's beautiful, you know. A sign of the battle you're fighting. And winning."

"I'll do that, thank you."

Before the evening was over, they had settled on a day that coming week. Lexi was getting tired and said her goodbyes. She was scheduled to be at the hospital for her shift at six in the morning and it would be hard enough to get up and going as it was.

She climbed into her car and leaned her head back against the head rest. It had been a great evening — she'd needed that more than she had realized. She'd needed to be surrounded by family.

It would have been a perfect evening if Lance had been there.

The thought came out of left field and struck Lexi with such force that she sat up straight.

She missed Lance.

~

Lance's phone buzzed and he picked it up to see a text from Lexi. He had hoped she might let him know how the family dinner went. All evening, he'd tried to keep busy watching television or doing anything else he could to pass the time. He tossed the remote control on the couch beside him and opened the text message.

"I just got home from dinner. It went pretty well. Thanks again for giving Tuck a heads up."

"You're welcome. I saw the picture of you and Grams. That was awesome. How are you feeling?"

"I'm good, thanks."

There was a pause and then another text from her.

"I missed you."

He tapped on the green symbol next to her name and waited as the phone rang. He leaned back into the cushions and let her voice wash over him. "Hey, you."

Lance smiled. "I missed you, too."

"How was your night?"

"Long." He hadn't been able to take his mind off Lexi, wondering how things were going. "But I got a lot of work done today and that always feels good."

"Do you still miss being a cop?"

"During the day sometimes. But I don't miss the late-night call outs." He laid down on his couch, propping his head on the arm. "You have a shift tomorrow, right?"

"Yes. My schedule has been all over the place lately. I'm going to check and see what I can do about this weekend."

"We probably won't see each other much this week, then."

Lexi was silent for a moment and he checked the screen to make sure their call hadn't disconnected. "Are you okay?"

"Yeah. You know, if you wanted to come by for lunch one day, that wouldn't be a bad thing."

He chuckled, a smile on his face and anticipation welling up in his chest. "I bet we can arrange that. How about Wednesday?"

"Wednesday sounds great. Can I text you about the time that morning?"

"Absolutely. You know you can call me whenever you want, right?"

"I do. Thanks, Lance. The same goes for you."

"Thanks. I'll see you in a few days."

"Have a good night."

"You, too."

He waited for her to hang up before turning his screen off.

Lexi had missed him and suggested they have lunch together that week. Oh, yeah. Life was good.

~

"Okay. What happened?"

Lance barely had the chance to slide into the booth across from Tuck Monday morning before the words had left his best friend's mouth.

"Excuse me?"

"I can tell something's changed and you know you want to tell me. Come on, out with it."

Lance shook his head. "You're scary sometimes. Seriously. Have you thought about a career with the FBI? Or maybe the secret service?"

"I've considered it. But I've heard their vacation packages are terrible." Tuck gave him his best guise of innocence.

Lance wadded up a napkin and tossed it at him.

The waitress arrived with their drinks and they placed their breakfast orders.

As soon as she walked away, Tuck was pinning him down with that look of his, the one that almost always got suspects to crack under pressure.

Lance crossed his arms.

His friend stared at him, looking for clues. His eyes widened. "Lexi was acting differently at dinner. You kissed her, didn't you?"

Schooling his features, Lance reached nonchalantly for his glass of orange juice.

Tuck threw his head back and laughed. "It's about time, man."

~

Lexi had promised to stop by Laurie's

photography studio before starting her afternoon shift at the hospital on Monday. She'd loved how the photos from the first session turned out and felt more relaxed this time around.

Laurie was a gifted photographer and had a way of making the subjects of her photos be themselves. She believed there was a time and place for posed photos. But an image showing the true personality of the person in it said so much more.

A bell above the door announced her presence. Laurie peeked at her from the other side of a backdrop she was raising back into position.

"Hey, Lexi! Right on time!" She finished her task and brushed some dust off of her pants. "How's your day going?"

"My shift starts in an hour, but I'm off to a good start."

"I don't know how you deal with the different schedules. It would drive me insane. Does your body ever have a hard time figuring out when it should sleep?"

Lexi helped her move two larger props out of the middle of the floor and to a space against one wall.

"In the beginning it did. But now, unless something major is going on, I'm tired by the time I get home and my body has no choice but to sleep."

Laurie got a beautiful wooden chair and placed it near a window at the front of the studio. Lexi remembered seeing a cabinet or a bookshelf near there but the space was empty now.

"Tell me where you want me."

She watched as Laurie got everything set up. She brought out a couple of different lengths of cloth, expertly draping a brown one around Lexi's body until it resembled a dress.

With a satisfied smile she gave a nod. "Perfect. It's almost the exact same color as your eyes."

Lexi thought the session went well. Laurie coached her and suggested different things to her, but none of it felt unnatural. Twenty minutes later, the session was finished.

"I can't wait to see what you do with this."

Laurie smiled at her. "I'll process them and try to get some back to you by the end of the week."

"That sounds perfect. I know you have a lot of sessions this week. Don't feel rushed." She reached out to hug her sister-in-law. "I'm very thankful for you."

"I feel the same way about you."

They said their goodbyes and Lexi headed to the hospital.

She was feeling pretty off today. Not only did she feel tired, but dizzy and a little euphoric. She'd read that the reduction in white blood cell counts could cause her body's responses. She wasn't overly concerned. Still, it was distracting.

Once she got to the hospital, she changed into her scrubs and headed to the break room.

By now, all of her coworkers knew about her fight with ovarian cancer. Most treated her normally. She had two coworkers come up to share their own experiences. A few of the others had looked at her as though they expected her to keel over at any moment.

Finnegan hadn't spoken with her since she'd confronted him with the truth last week. When she ran into him, she got the polite hello. They went their separate ways, which suited Lexi just fine. Because if a man was going to be the focus of her thoughts, there was no doubt it was Lance.

His name brought a smile to her face and a bounce to her step as she left the coffee brewing in the break room and headed for the nurse's station.

It was time to get to work.

~

Lance had his cell phone to one ear, his microwaved meal forgotten in front of him as he chatted with Lexi.

"I went over my schedule at the hospital. I had to pull a few strings and trade shifts with a couple of people, but I'm free to go to the renaissance fair."

Thinking about spending the weekend with her made Lance's day. "That's great! I hope it wasn't too much trouble."

"No, it'll be fine. I'll work a double shift so I can get off at 6 a.m. Friday morning and won't go back to work again until 6 Sunday night."

He was glad they would have all day at the fair. But he hated it when she worked double shifts. "You'll be exhausted."

"Nah. I'll go home and sleep a few hours. Then, as long as you don't mind if I sleep a couple more on the way there, I'll be fine."

"I get to drive you down to Magnolia?" The thought put a smile on his face.

"I should have asked if you were going with your parents or your sisters. I didn't even…"

"Lex."

"Yeah?"

"I was hoping to drive with you."

"Okay. I'm glad."

Lance could imagine the blush creeping into her cheeks and wished he could see it for himself.

They worked out a few more details. Lexi was hesitant to go in a full renaissance outfit and Lance didn't even have one anymore. They decided to dress normally and go to enjoy the shows and demonstrations.

By the time they said their goodnights, Lance's heart was light.

Chapter Fourteen

Lance helped Lexi put her rolling suitcase in the back of his Jeep and opened the door for her. She put on her seat belt, excited for the weekend. It'd been a while since she'd gone out of town for anything fun. She didn't realize how much she needed this until now.

She kicked her shoes off for the long drive. "I've got almost forty-eight hours before I have to work again. I'm more than ready for this."

"Me, too." He looked at her, a grin on his face.

"Tell me about the sisters I'm going to meet today."

They spent the majority of the drive talking about family, funny things that happened at previous renaissance fairs Lance had been to, and eating sandwiches along the way. By the time they got to the hotel, it was almost nine. He had booked hotel rooms down the same hall making it easy for them to all connect. The other members of his family were already at a restaurant next door and had texted to let Lance know. He and Lexi deposited their things in their rooms and walked back down the hall to the elevator.

The door closed. Lance took one of her hands in his and rested his other on the rail against the wall behind her. "I may not get the chance to do this again before we leave." His voice was husky, his intentions clear.

Lexi took in a deep breath. When she didn't object, he kissed her. Every other thought drifted away as she relished the feel of his lips against hers in a kiss she wouldn't forget for a long time to come.

The chime of the elevator announced their arrival. Lance moved back, but he moved his arm to encircle her waist as they stepped into the lobby.

Lexi's legs felt weak as she worked to even her breathing. She tried to get her thoughts in order before they reached the restaurant.

As soon as they entered, Lexi spotted the Davenports waving them over. The feel of Lance's hand on her lower back reassured her, relieving an onslaught of nerves.

"Hey, everyone!" Lance gave hugs all the way around the table. Then he turned and made introductions.

Lexi greeted Peter and Vera again with a wave and a smile. His sister, Gwen, was a younger version of Vera. She was holding hands with Zane, her husband of a few months. Beth, the youngest Davenport sibling, resembled Lance in some ways. His family seemed friendly and Lexi was happy to join them at the table, sitting between Lance and Vera.

"We're happy you could join us, Lexi," Vera said, a

sincere smile on her face. "We remember meeting you a few times, but never had much opportunity to visit."

"I remember, ma'am. It was at Lance's high school graduation and then again, when he and Tuck graduated from the police academy. I'm sure we've run into each other at least a time or two since."

"Yes, I think you're right. And those events are always busy, it's hard to visit with too many people. Have you ever been to a renaissance fair before?"

"No, ma'am. I sure haven't."

"Please, call me Vera." She took a drink of her lemonade. "And I'm sure you'll enjoy it. Who knows, maybe you'll be a new fan and can go with us every year to the one in Oklahoma."

Lexi glanced at Lance and back to his mom. "I'm sure I'll have fun. I think my sister-in-law, Laurie, was a little jealous. She's a photographer and said she would love to take photos of all the different costumes people wear."

Zane spoke from across the table. "This will be my first renaissance fair, too. The good news, is they have alcohol there if we need that to get through the day."

He winked and Gwen elbowed him hard in the ribs. "No one knows you well enough yet for you to joke like that," she chided, blushing all the way to the roots of her hair. "He's kidding."

Lexi chuckled. Most of the dinner, she listened to the discussions that floated around her. How they had all intended to bring costumes and everything and dress up like they used to, but they hadn't had enough time to prepare. They would have to go and not worry about blending in this year. Then they would have months to put together their costumes for the

Oklahoma fair in May.

Secretly, Lexi was just as glad. For her first renaissance fair, she would rather play it safe.

Dinner wound down and people headed back to the hotel. The plan was to meet in the lobby for the continental breakfast at half past seven, that way they could be at the fair when doors opened at nine.

Everyone intended to stay the entire day until it closed with fireworks at nine that evening.

Lance walked her to her hotel room door. "Are you ready for tomorrow?"

She raised an eyebrow. "Sounds like I'd better be." She gave him a teasing smile. "It'll be fun."

"Definitely." He gave her an all-too-brief kiss. "I'll see you in the morning."

~

There was already a crowd when they arrived at the fairgrounds the next morning. Lance held onto Lexi's hand as they got their tickets and headed through the gates. With this many people, it would be easy to get separated.

"Wow, you can rent costumes?" Lexi's voice was incredulous as they walked down a street with storefronts on either side. Each one designed and decorated to fit the period. He noted the one she was referring to with fancy dresses hanging in the window.

"Dressing up in costume is a big thing at fairs like this," Vera said. "We always did. It makes you feel like you're part of it."

Lance watched as his dad maneuvered his walker through the crowd.

He knew Peter had hesitated in taking it, but with

all the walking they would do today, Vera had insisted. It helped him move, but it also provided a chair for him to sit on when they stopped or when he needed a rest.

That Peter Davenport needed a walker at all bothered Lance.

His mind shifted to the woman walking beside him. She was dressed in capris and a blouse that flowed over her hips. She had chosen a scarf that went well with the blouse and brought out the color in her cheeks. They'd all brought jackets in case they needed them, but left them in the vehicles since warm weather was predicted. He gently squeezed her hand and took in a deep breath. She smelled like lavender and summer.

Lance enjoyed the day, seeing a renaissance fair through the eyes of someone who was there for the first time. Lexi seemed to have the most fun watching the jousting and sword fights.

That evening, Peter was getting tired. He and Vera found a spot to sit and listen to some entertainment. The rest of them perused the shops.

"Check these out, Lance!"

Lexi tugged on his hand to stop him in front of the glass blowing display. There was a man who was creating a vase as they watched, with many other pieces set up on tables and shelves.

"They are beautiful," he commented. The way the guy was creating the vase with such precise and delicate movements was mesmerizing.

Lexi reached out and touched a glass ball the size of her palm. The shades of blue and white swirled inside in infinite patterns. "It reminds me of the ocean."

A woman in period clothing walked up to the table. "You can pick it up if you'd like."

Letting go of Lance's hand, Lexi lifted the ball and cupped it in her hands. "It's much lighter than I thought it would be. It's amazing how detailed it is." She set it back down again. She watched the man working with the glass. "You are talented."

He gave a short nod. "Thank you, My Lady."

Beth, Gwen, and Zane joined them. "Is anyone else getting hungry?" Gwen asked.

They decided they were.

Beth took hold of both Gwen and Lexi's arms. "I think we girls should go powder our noses and meet you guys over by Mom and Dad."

Lance watched as the women disappeared into the crowd. He turned to Zane. "Gwen seems happy. I'm glad for both of you."

"I appreciate that. Lexi seems great," Zane commented as they made their way back to where they'd left Peter and Vera.

"She is. I thank God every day she's in my life."

~

Lexi liked Lance's sisters. They were both carefree and walked through the fair liked they owned the place. Which was good, because Lexi still felt very much like a tourist, and a lost one at that if they hadn't been there to steer her in the right direction.

"I'm glad you came with us this weekend," Gwen said as they picked their way through the crowd. "Mom and Dad appreciate it when the significant others join in family events."

Lexi wanted to object about the significant other

comment, but Beth was already talking. "It's true. They weren't sure about Zane until he fixed Mom's car right after Christmas."

"That was sweet of him," Lexi agreed.

Gwen chuckled. "You're the first woman Lance has ever brought home." Her face became more serious. "This year has been rough for Dad with his stroke and all. There have been two good things that have come out of it, though. Lance took over the carpentry shop and he's interested in you."

"I imagine Peter was relieved to see the carpentry shop remain open."

Beth nodded. "He was. That wasn't the only thing that mattered. It's Davenport Carpentry. It was Grandpa's place before it was his. Dad wanted nothing more than for it to continue to stay in the family."

Lexi hadn't realized the shop had been in the family that long. "If Lance hadn't been able to take over, is there no one else who could do it?"

Gwen spotted the rest of their party ahead and waved to them. "Dad was the only son in his family, like Lance is the only son in ours. He's the last Davenport. If Lance hadn't taken over the shop that would have been the end of it."

Lexi continued walking with them, their voices fading to the background. Her legs felt numb and her mouth went dry.

Lance was the last Davenport man in his family. And he was interested in her — a woman who couldn't give him children, much less a son to carry on the family name. Did his parents know any of that? Would they have been so kind if they had?

The last week with Lance had been amazing. She'd

let her guard down. The worst part was she'd known better. She should have listened to her gut and insisted she and Lance stay friends.

~

Lance polished off the last of his turkey leg and threw the bone in a nearby trash barrel. He wiped his hands off on a paper towel and tossed that, too.

"Wow, this is good." Lexi took another bite out of the fried chicken breast on a stick. "I'll have to search around online and get a batter recipe. I want to try making some of these."

"You should make them for Tuck. He'd love it."

"Yes, he would. Though I would have to make a dozen of them just for him."

She chuckled. Her gaze flitted from his face to the musicians playing across the square.

A breeze was picking up now that the sun had set. Another forty minutes and they would end the evening with fireworks before heading back to the hotel.

Sitting out under the stars was the perfect way to end the day.

Peter was talking about how he'd liked one of the booths they'd seen. It featured wooden items that had been decorated using wood burning.

"I was thinking, Lance. Maybe I could learn how to do that. I could add details to some of your work."

"I'd like that, Dad. It's a great idea."

The light in Peter's eyes as he talked about his new hobby in the making had his whole family excited for him.

Vera shifted closer to her son. "You were right.

This was what he needed. Thank you."

Lance put an arm around her. "I'm glad he's finding another focus."

Lexi was laughing with Beth. Lance leaned back against some bricks behind him and enjoyed watching her. The breeze was blowing her scarf around her shoulders. She brushed it back behind her with those long, delicate fingers.

He could watch her laugh like that for hours.

A few minutes later, he moved to Lexi's side. "Is there anything else you need before the fireworks start?"

"No, thank you. I'm good."

She smiled at him, but there was something he couldn't quite put his finger on. He'd been wondering about it for a couple of hours now. "Are you okay?"

"I'm getting tired. It's been a lot of fun and I'm glad I came. But I'll be glad to get back to the hotel."

"I should have offered to take you back early."

She shook her head. "I'm fine, Lance. I wouldn't have wanted to miss the fireworks."

He reached for her hand and tugged her to his side. "I'm glad you came, too." He kissed her temple.

The sky lit up with blue and red as appreciative cheers erupted from the crowd. Lexi moved to sit on a low brick wall behind them. He joined her, putting an arm around her shoulders.

The fireworks display intensified.

"They are beautiful," Lexi said.

They weren't nearly as beautiful as the woman sitting next to him.

~

Lexi wanted to lean into Lance's strength and warmth so desperately that it hurt. She closed her eyes against the pain that was growing in her heart. How was she going to act normal tomorrow during the drive home?

She had to talk to him. She would wait until they got back to her apartment, because the thought of riding for five hours together after that was more than she could handle.

Exhausted in every way, she tried to focus on the fireworks. On the way back to the hotel, she made small talk about the different booths and costumes.

When she escaped to her hotel room, she collapsed onto her bed in tears.

Chapter Fifteen

The moment Lexi opened her eyes Sunday morning, dread turned her stomach into knots. She worked to pack all of her things back into her rolling bag. How was she going to tell Lance?

No matter what she came up with, all she could picture was a look of hurt in his eyes. That alone made her want to cry. Again.

It would be worse, though, in another week or a month. Each day she spent with Lance made her feel more whole and safe than the day before. She was losing her heart to him.

She had to tell him they needed space. Convince him that there was someone else out there for him who could give him everything he needed in a family.

Even if it meant breaking her own heart to do it.

When she had her bag ready to go, she squared her shoulders and took a deep breath. She could do this. She could get through the next five or six hours.

Lexi was the last of their group to arrive for

breakfast. Lance had saved her a seat and a blueberry muffin.

"I noticed you had one yesterday and this was the last. I figured I would grab it for you."

Why did the man have to be so perfect?

"Thank you, that was thoughtful."

She got herself a glass of apple juice and sat next to him to eat her muffin. Conversation was light and soon they were getting in their vehicles to drive back home again.

Lexi wasn't sure if it would be easier or harder to be alone with him now.

Lance checked his mirror, merged onto the highway, and cast a smile her way. "I think that was good for Dad. I haven't seen him so happy in a long time."

"He seemed to enjoy himself. Your whole family did. I think it'll be good for all of you to make this a yearly tradition."

"So do I." He reached over and took her hand. "Who knows, maybe you'll be there with us next year, too."

She was trying to figure out how to respond to that and took too long. He squeezed her hand gently. "What's up?"

Lexi rubbed her face with one hand. "I'm exhausted. Do you mind if I close my eyes and take a rest for a few minutes?"

"Of course not." He kissed her knuckles and released her hand.

She willed herself to fall asleep. If only her heart would stop aching in her chest.

~

By the time they got back to Kitner, everything in Lance told him something was wrong and Lexi wasn't talking about it. As he pulled to a stop in front of her apartment, he noticed tears in her eyes before she got out of the Jeep.

He retrieved her bag and carried it to her door.

"You're worrying me, Lex. What's going on?"

"Lance, this weekend was great. You're amazing, but…"

He wasn't about to let her finish. "No, no, no. Honey, what happened? I thought everything went well. Did my parents say anything to you? My sisters?" He put his hands on her shoulders and desperately tried to figure out what might have happened over the last day and a half.

"No, they were great. Your family's wonderful." She lifted her eyes to his, a tear sliding down her cheek. "You've become my best friend, Lance. I am thankful for that and it hurts to think I might have ruined it."

"You haven't ruined anything. Lex, I lo…"

"Don't." She placed a hand on his chest, tears chasing each other down her face. "Don't say it. I'm not the right woman for you. You'll meet her someday. And when you do, you'll know I was right."

She might as well have thrust a knife into his heart and turned it. There had to be a way he could fix this — convince her she was the only one for him. That his life wasn't complete without her. "Let's go inside and talk." He reached for her hand and turned towards the door.

"Lance, you won't change my mind. I hate myself for dumping this on you now after all you've done for me. But I think you should go. I think it'll be better for both of us if you do."

Lance was feeling a sense of panic rise in his chest. He reached for her hand. "Don't push me away, Lex. Talk to me."

"Good night, Lance."

The half-smile she gave him was full of regret. She disappeared into her apartment, leaving Lance feeling as though he'd had a hole punched into his chest.

~

"Do you have a minute?" Tuck's voice at the shop door startled Lance and he turned the sander off, setting it down.

"Sure." He stood. "What's going on?"

"First, you canceled our breakfast yesterday. Then I find out Lexi is upset and won't tell anyone why. What'd you do to my sister?" Tuck's face was about as serious as Lance had ever seen it.

Lance stood and held his hands out to his side. "Man, if I knew what was going on I would tell you. Things were great and we had a lot of fun at the renaissance fair. That night she was acting a little odd but I thought she was tired." The whole thing replayed in his head like it had a thousand times in the last day. His chest hurt. "She was upset when I took her home on Sunday. She insisted she wasn't the right woman for me and that was all I could get out of her. Now she won't return my calls."

Tuck stared at him for a moment. "I'd thought you guys had moved past the kids thing."

"I thought we had, too. This is killing me. I wish she would talk to me."

"I tried to catch her this morning and she's not talking to anyone else, either. This is about Lexi, Lance. She can be incredibly stubborn. Which is a good trait to have when she's trying to accomplish something or fight cancer. But it makes it really difficult to convince her when she's wrong. Trust me, I know. Don't blame yourself."

"It's hard not to." He pointed an accusing finger at Tuck. "And you're scary when you're trying to figure out what's going on with your sisters. I wouldn't want to be on your bad side."

Tuck laughed and gave him a friendly shove. Determination replaced his smile. "What are your intentions towards Lexi?"

Lance blinked at him. "Look, I…"

"Answer the question."

"I'm in love with her. Maybe I always have been. I can't imagine living the rest of my life without her."

With a quick nod, Tuck showed his approval. "Don't let her pull away from you."

"I can't even get her to see me right now."

"Find a way. She's been through a lot lately and maybe it's all caught up with her."

Lance leaned against one of the support beams and let out a forceful breath of air. Tuck might be right. "I guess we all have a breaking point." He stared his best friend in the eye. "I'm not giving up on her."

"Good."

~

Lexi's last couple of days had been rough. Add that it was Wednesday and normally she would have seen Lance for lunch, and it made the day even worse.

When she pulled up to her apartment and saw his Jeep parked out front, she wanted to turn around and leave. Instead, she took in a deep breath, squared her shoulders, and walked to her door.

Lance stood from the spot where he'd been sitting. "I hate to ambush you like this, Lex, but you wouldn't answer my phone calls."

"This isn't a good time. I'm coming off back-to-back shifts."

"You tell me when we can talk and I'll be there."

She passed her hand over her eyes, willing herself to think through the pounding in her head. "I don't know."

Her phone rang and she pulled it out of her pocket. It was Tuck's number and she promptly answered it. "Hey, Tuck. What's up?"

"I only have a minute, Lexi. It came over the scanner a moment ago. There's a fire at Mom's house. I don't know how bad it is. I have to go but wanted to call you first."

"No! Okay. Go. I'll see you there." She hung up the phone to find Lance's concerned gaze on her. "Mom's house is on fire. I have to get over there. What if someone's hurt?"

Lance took her elbow and steered her towards his Jeep.

"I'll drive."

Lexi started to object, but he cut her off. "You just said you got off after working a double shift. You're in no condition to drive over there. Please, let me take you."

She nodded her agreement. He was right. She could barely think, let alone drive, right now. She rode in the passenger seat, leaning forward, her body tense.

Lance kept telling her about how it might be a minor fire and how they shouldn't jump to conclusions. She knew he was right, but couldn't make herself voice any of what was going through her head.

~

Lance drove to the Chandler house as fast as he could, his hands clenching the steering wheel — a close comparison to how his stomach was feeling at the moment. He tried not to think about the four people who lived in that house and where they might be right now.

The fire engine out front indicated they'd reached their destination before he ever saw the house itself. It was a relief to see the front was intact when he'd worried the whole thing would be engulfed in flames.

He could tell Lexi had spotted her family and she had released her seatbelt as he put the Jeep in park. She was running to them before he'd gotten out of the vehicle himself.

Lexi was hugging both Patty and Grams by the time he got there. "I'm glad you're both okay. What happened?"

"I don't know." Grams' face was creased with worry. "It started in the kitchen. I had made dinner fifteen minutes before. I don't know if it was something I did or forgot to do."

"Now, Mom. Don't blame yourself. We don't know anything yet." Patty put an arm around Grams.

Lexi cast furtive glances around her. "Where are Serenity and Gideon?"

"They weren't here, praise God. We ran out of milk and they ran to the store." Patty kept one hand on Grams' shoulder. "Mom, you need to sit down for a while."

Lance held a hand out. "I've got it." He jogged around to the back porch. Smoke was still seeping through the broken windows and he spotted firemen inside. He grabbed two folding chairs off the deck and carried them back up front. After he set them up, he helped Grams take a seat. He offered the other to both Patty and Lexi. The Chandler women turned him down. "Have you seen Tuck?"

Patty nodded. "He's around here somewhere."

Oh good, something he could do. He hated feeling helpless.

"I'll go locate him and see what I can find out. I'll be back as quickly as I can." He gave Lexi's arm a squeeze and headed for the fire engine. He found Tuck on the other side, talking to three firefighters.

Tuck gave him a grateful nod and waved him over.

Lance joined him as the firemen moved away.

"What happened?"

"They're going to investigate further, but it looks like one of the stove burners was on. Paper towels ended up on the burner or near it. They caught fire, it spread to the dish towel, and it continued from there." Tuck ran his fingers through his hair. "It was an accident, plain and simple."

"Praise God no one was hurt." Lance studied the house. From the front, you wouldn't know anything had happened. "Can we go inside?"

"Yes. They said we can go in and see the damage, but no one can stay in it until the smoke dissipates. It could take several days, so we'll need to get some things for everyone. Thankfully, it was just the kitchen that was damaged by fire or smoke."

Lance nodded. "It could have been much worse. Have you called Serenity?"

"Her phone went right to voicemail. I'm thinking it's dead. I need to go by the store and find…"

"Tuck! Tuck!"

The voice behind them drew their attention to the object of their conversation. She was running towards them, Gideon in tow.

"Serenity, everyone's okay." Tuck reached out to take Gideon's hand.

"What happened?"

Lance nodded towards the others. "We were about to go back and let them know."

The four of them joined Grams, Patty, and Lexi. The ladies listened as Tuck repeated what he had told Lance.

Grams and Patty were both silent, tears streaming down their faces.

"I left that burner on," Grams said, her voice barely above a whisper.

Patty put an arm around her. "No. I cleaned up after lunch. I put the paper towels on the stove while I was wiping off the counters. Why didn't I check to make sure the burners were turned off?"

The two women went to hug each other, their tears flowing.

Lexi reached out and gently took each of them by an arm, turning them to look at her. "It was an accident. An unfortunate one. But that's all it was. It could have happened to any of us. Taking blame and reliving it won't help. No one was injured and that's what we need to focus on. The rest of the house was spared. We need to move forward."

They regarded each other and nodded.

"Good. Now, Tuck said they told us we could go in. Let's go take a look at the damage and put together a game plan." She smiled at Gideon and ruffled his hair. "No one's staying in a hotel. Between Tuck and I, there will be places for all of you to sleep."

Tuck nodded in agreement. "We'll get this figured out."

Lance's chest swelled with pride as he watched Lexi step up and put her family at ease in the middle of a crisis.

It was clear why she became a nurse. She'd always had a knack for taking care of other people. She was good at it, too.

Her eyes sought his and she gave him a determined smile. Yes, he was proud to know this beautiful woman who, along with Tuck, was leading her family into their home.

The smell of smoke burned his nostrils as he stepped into the living room. Together, they approached the kitchen and stopped at the door. It was almost unrecognizable. The fire had left behind gruesome black streaks on the walls and charred appliances. The floor was covered with layers of ash and water. Lance's eyes went to the back door. It was open and the glass in the windows had been knocked out when the firefighters had battled the blaze.

In the midst of all that damage, one object seemed to draw everyone's attention. The kitchen table.

Lance knew the story well. Grams' late husband, Nicholas, had crafted the table with his own hands before Patty was born. Many people who knew the

Chandler family admired the table and tried to convince Nicholas to make and sell tables like it. He'd always refused. He gave it to Grams one Christmas and it had been the centerpiece in the Chandler home ever since.

Now, the half of the table closest to the stove had black streaks that stretched like evil fingers infecting the beautiful wood. The fire had eaten away at one corner. The other half of the table had been spared from the flames, but it was covered with water and ash.

Chapter Sixteen

The moment she spotted the table, Lexi's breath whooshed from her lungs. Her body tense, she put a hand against her chest, fingers splayed near her neck.

Grams was holding her locket. The brass heart hung from a matching chain. She pressed her lips to the three-dimensional compass on the surface.

Lexi could picture the photo of Gramps inside and knew that Grams was in shock. The table was her favorite possession — besides the locket — that he had given to her.

Lexi could only imagine the emotions that must be going through her right now. Someone walked up behind Lexi and placed a hand on her shoulder. She glanced back to find Lance, his face a picture of sympathy. She turned back to the table, but allowed herself to take what strength she could from his touch and resisted the urge to lean into him.

The sorrow in the group dripped like the ashen

water from the walls.

"Gideon!"

Serenity reached for her son who had broken away from the rest of them. He was too quick and dashed into the kitchen towards the table. He stooped to pick an object up off the floor.

Lexi watched with the others as he made his way to the fridge. He placed a magnet on the small portion of the fridge that was still smooth. It was a magnet they'd ordered online after the last family portrait. Somehow, despite what had occurred in the kitchen, it seemed to be untouched.

Gideon stood back and grinned, satisfaction on his face, as the images in the photo smiled back at him. The devastation around him didn't matter as long as that picture was where it needed to be.

It was that moment when tears found their way to Lexi's eyes. She sniffed at the same time that Serenity did.

"It's stuff." Grams drew herself up to her full height and tucked the locket inside her blouse. "The fridge. That stove. The walls. They're only things. The table didn't make this family. It's the family that made this table special. And we're all here. Together."

Gideon rejoined them and Patty put her arms around him, kissing his head. "She's right. We have so many things to be thankful for."

Lexi blinked away the moisture and cleared her throat. "All right, everyone. I think that's about all the sappiness I can take today. Let's get what you all need for a few days and meet back down here."

They did as she suggested and agreed to go to Tuck's house to get everything figured out. They were about to leave when Grams carried a towel she'd retrieved from the bathroom into the kitchen. Lovingly, she wiped all the water and ash off the table, going over it again one more time to make sure it was clean and dry.

No one said anything as they watched her. When she folded the towel and left it hanging over a chair, Lexi and Serenity went forward to each give her a kiss on the cheek.

"We love you, Grams," Lexi whispered near her ear.

Grams put an arm around each of them. "I love you girls, too."

When they got to Tuck's house, Laurie met them at the door, welcoming them all with hugs. "I have cookies, juice, cold water, and tea in the kitchen if anyone needs a snack."

Lexi accepted the hug. "You're Wonder Woman having all of this ready like that. Thank you."

Gideon raced past them as Lance chased after him while growling like a bear. Squeals emanated from the kitchen. The women laughed.

As they polished off the cookies, the sounds of Lexi's family laughing around her was like a salve on an open wound.

At the end of the evening, they decided that Patty and Grams would stay with Tuck and Laurie. They had more room and better beds for them to sleep on.

Serenity and Gideon would stay with Lexi. She had the couch Serenity could sleep on and they grabbed Gideon's sleeping bag and pillow so he would be fine on the floor for a few nights.

Lexi yawned widely for the tenth time. She was past the point of being spent. Between only hours of broken sleep and then the drama of the fire, she was sure she could sleep for a day.

"You desperately need some rest." Lance moved to stand next to her as though he were afraid she might collapse. "If you guys are ready, you should head back to your place."

Lexi glanced at Serenity who nodded.

"I think that's a good idea."

"Do you want me to drive you home?"

Serenity helped Gideon don his backpack. "I have room in my car for Lexi."

Lexi offered Lance a tired smile. "You've gone above and beyond today. I'll go back with Serenity." She stepped closer to him and lowered her voice a little. "Thank you for everything. Your support meant a lot to all of us."

He softly touched the back of his fingers to her cheek. "I'm glad I could be here for you."

~

The kitchen at the Chandler house was a real mess. Lance had volunteered to go over with Tuck the next day to take inventory. They'd arranged for someone to get the water mess cleaned up. They also called in an expert to give them an idea of what it would cost to gut that part of the kitchen and rebuild it. It cost more, but they'd been fortunate to find a company that could get started that week.

Lance had told Grams he would move the table back to his workshop.

Now he stood examining it. The burned half of the table was even worse than he thought it would be. When he first saw it, he had hoped that he might be able to sand out some of the light charring and then stain or paint it. But the damage was much more severe. That half of the table would not be salvageable.

He knew that Grams would be brokenhearted, though how the older woman pulled herself together the day before would fill anyone with admiration.

He knew Lexi took after her Grams.

That brought a smile to his face.

He reached a hand out, touching the surface of the table. He could imagine Nicholas spending hours and hours working on it, the image of his wife's happy face when she saw it keeping him going.

Had he imagined his children eating at the table as they grew up? What about his grandchildren?

Lance would find a way to take what was left of that table and turn it into something Grams could hold onto and continue to pass down through the generations.

There was a soft knock at the entrance to the shop. When he saw who it was, he forgot the pad of paper and pencil he'd been holding.

"Avalon! Are you okay?"

His sister, Avalon, stood there, guilt all over her face. She'd never been good at hiding her emotions, not even when they were kids. It made her even more emotional when everyone else could read her like a book.

"I'm fine, Lance. Can't your sister come home for a visit?"

"Out of the blue after living in Arizona the last two years? Seems a little fishy."

She shot him a glare so cold he could have sworn the temperature had decreased in the shop ten degrees.

He stood and went forward, engulfing her in a brotherly hug. "I'm kidding, Avalon. It's good to see you. What brings you to good old Texas?"

Avalon gave him another firm stare but took a seat on the chair in the corner. "I'm thinking about moving back."

His eyebrows rose. Avalon had left home as soon as she'd graduated from high school. She'd gone to college in Arizona, only to drop out her sophomore year, saying college wasn't for her. She stayed in Arizona, working odd jobs that none of them could seem to keep up with. He wasn't even sure what town she claimed to be home.

She'd needed her space and while it was hard on their parents, they respected her decisions, and she'd always seemed happy.

Something had to have changed for her to come home like this.

"What happened?"

Moisture gathered in his younger sister's eyes and the part of him that always felt protective of his siblings came to the surface. He pulled a chair closer to her and sat down.

"What's wrong, Avalon? Do I need to fly to Arizona and hunt someone down?"

That got a giggle. She swiped at her eyes and took a steadying breath. "I screwed up. Big time."

He stayed silent, waiting for her to open up and tell him what was going on.

"I'm married, Lance. And last week, I said I needed space. That's why I'm here. To think."

That was the last thing he expected her to say. Well, outside of a declaration about overtaking a country. He knew his mouth was hanging open.

"You're WHAT?"

"His name is Duke. We got married in July." She stopped.

"Was he abusive? Did he hit you? He sounds like a guy that would hit a woman."

"No!" Avalon stood, too, and placed a hand on his chest. "He's a gentleman. He'd never do something like that."

"Then why on earth are you leaving him? It all seems way too rushed. Ending a marriage is as big of a decision as beginning one."

"I'm not leaving him. I needed space to think, and he did, too."

"If you're married and having trouble, I don't think going out of state is the way to handle things." His voice relayed the shock he felt. The tension was palpable.

"Right. You're a happily married man — of course you know what you're talking about." The words dripped sarcasm.

"Then why did you come to me? Why not go talk to Marian? Or Gwen? Or Mom?"

Avalon collapsed onto the chair again, covering her face with her hands as she moaned. "I don't know. Because maybe their marriages are too happy."

Lance covered his mouth with his hand, blowing air against it. He ran his hand across his goatee. He said a prayer for patience.

"Come here, Avalon."

She stood, her eyes widening when he reached and drew her into a bear hug. "What's that for?"

"Because I'm happy to see my little sister and I hate that I have no idea what's going on in your life and I can't make any judgments. I love you. I want you to be happy. And I want to help you." Her arms tightened around him with a fierceness that worried him. What had happened to her in the last few months?

~

Lexi woke up bleary-eyed. Which was never a good sign. She entered the kitchen to find Serenity and Gideon helping themselves to breakfast.

"Are you okay?" Serenity was studying her older sister.

"I'm ready for a vacation." She took a drink of orange juice.

"Have you considered working somewhere else?"

Lexi shook her head. "I love being a nurse. It's what I've always wanted to be."

"I'm not talking a change in profession. What about a change in employers? When we were at Gideon's last appointment at the pediatrician's office, the lady up front mentioned that they were trying to find another nurse to hire on there. I have no idea what kind of pay that is and how it might compare to the hospital. There have to be other nursing opportunities where you aren't working twelve hour shifts back-to-back."

There had been a time when Lexi would have balked at working anywhere but the hospital. But between being held at knifepoint back in February, her cancer, and now the fire, she couldn't deny that having a normal 9 to 5 job sounded wonderful.

"Thanks, Serenity. I'll think about it."

She turned her attention to Gideon, who was munching on cereal. "How are you doing, big guy?

Did you sleep well?"

He didn't respond, but he picked an apple out of the bowl on the table and handed it to her.

"Thank you. You knew just what I needed for breakfast." She pretended to gobble it all down in seconds. Gideon laughed at that and handed her another apple. She repeated the performance. After the third apple, she magically produced the first two again and juggled them. One by one, she placed them back in the bowl.

Serenity was smiling at them. "You are amazing with kids."

Yes, she was. Ironic since she would never have one of her own. Thinking about it made her heart ache. She'd have to focus on the kids she helped. Try to let it go. Maybe she would get a dog or two and become the neighborhood dog lady.

Yeah, that made sense. Because a houseful of dogs was precisely what she needed when she worked twelve hours a day.

Lexi gave them both goodbye hugs and left.

Serenity's suggestion kept popping up in her mind. It wasn't a bad one.

Wondering what Lance would think of the idea, she almost dialed his number out of habit. She realized what she was doing and shoved her phone back into her pocket again with a groan.

Her day was a long one and all Lexi could do was think about her job situation and how Lance had been there for her – for her whole family – the day before. She knew she was dwelling. But she'd managed to avoid doing that for the most part since her diagnosis and figured she was due.

Two hours before she was off for the night, they

had an emergency visit from a young woman who found a baby behind the dumpster near her house.

The baby boy was a newborn with over a foot of umbilical cord still attached, tied off with a shoestring. She'd found him wrapped in a bloody towel, alive but too weak to cry.

As Lexi and three others worked to stabilize him, she'd felt the anger build up inside her. How did people decide to take a new life and throw it away like garbage? Even if they couldn't handle a baby, there were safe places they could have taken him. What about all the couples out there who can't have children of their own and would give anything for that same baby.

The little one was severely dehydrated. They managed to get him started on fluids and took blood, sending it off for a gamut of tests. The pediatrician on call arrived and checked the baby's vitals. "Nice job, everyone. I'll take it from here."

Lexi watched as he and his team wheeled the baby away to the NICU. She prayed that God would give him strength to endure such a rough start to his life.

She was unable to get the baby boy out of her mind as she finished up her shift. Before leaving for home, Lexi took the elevator up to check on him.

It wasn't hard to locate the correct incubator. The pediatrician was nearby and he stepped forward when he saw her. "You guys did good work down there. Saved this little man's life."

Lexi lightly caressed the tiny hand that rested against his body. "He'll be okay then?"

"He should be. He's going to be here for a while, though. The police are still trying to locate his parents, and any other extended family, to piece together what happened."

Lexi nodded, unable to look away from that tiny face and those perfect lips that were making suckling motions as he slept.

The pediatrician moved to check on another patient and left her to stroke the baby's cheek.

Sometimes she missed being able to follow through on the patients she helped in the ER. Sure, many of them were treated and released during her shift. Most of the time, however, they were transferred somewhere else in the hospital and she never found out what happened to them.

It wouldn't hurt to check into other job possibilities like Serenity suggested.

She traced the baby's fingers one last time and started for home. When she arrived, she discovered she had a houseful. Serenity and Gideon were still there along with Lance and a woman she didn't recognize.

"Hi everyone," she greeted as she set her bag down and kicked her shoes off by the front door. This was one of the few nights she would have preferred to be alone. Having Lance there was an extra stress she didn't need right now. She took her surgical cap off and tossed it on top of her bag.

The others greeted her with waves and smiles. Gideon caught her by the hand and all but dragged her to the table. Once there, he hopped up and down, his face bright, as he motioned to the package of cookies decorated with colored candies.

"I like your thinking, mister." Lexi ruffled his hair as she watched Lance open the container and pass it around.

"Lexi, this is my sister, Avalon. Avalon, this is

Lexi."

The women shook hands.

Avalon was a little shorter than Lance. She had dark blonde hair that was straight and came to the middle of her back. When she smiled, Avalon's face revealed two deep dimples that added to the youthful appearance of her face.

"It's nice to meet you," Lexi said. "What brings you to Kitner?"

Avalon shrugged, giving Lance a sideways glance that had Lexi wondering what it meant. "I'm visiting my big brother for a few days. I needed to get out of town."

"Well, I'm sure your family is happy to have you here." Lexi spotted pizza boxes on the counter. "And God bless whoever brought the food."

They all ate in comfortable conversation. Lexi enjoyed the food but was so blasted tired she had a hard time focusing or visiting. Once, Lance caught her eye and mouthed, "Are you okay?"

She gave him a quick nod but he didn't seem convinced.

Lexi stepped into the kitchen to throw her paper plate away and snag another cookie. She heard footsteps behind her and knew Lance had followed her. How she longed to feel his strong arms around her right now.

"I'm worried about you, Lex."

"I'm fine. It was a rough day at work. Someone found a newborn discarded near a dumpster. We were able to stabilize him, but it was a close call. There are days when the world seems royally messed up."

"That baby was lucky to have you on his side. Is he going to be okay?"

"He should be. What a really cruddy way to enter the world." Her eyes filled with tears. He must have been able to hear it in her voice because he turned her to face him.

"God used you and your skills to save him. There's a lot to rejoice about. We may not know what that baby's future holds. Maybe he had to go through what he did because he was born into an abusive situation. All so that he'll end up in the loving home he deserves."

Lexi hadn't thought about it that way. His words were like a balm to her heart. "Thank you," she whispered. "You always seem to know the right thing to say."

"Not always." Lance's eyes were sad as he studied her. "I miss you."

"Lance, don't."

He was about to say something else when Avalon came into the kitchen.

"I needed another cookie."

"Right over here." Lexi picked up the container and held it out to her.

Avalon took one and held it up to her. "Thank you very much."

"You're welcome."

Lexi watched her leave before turning to Lance. "Thank you for bringing dinner tonight."

"You're welcome. I know you've had a long day. Avalon and I are going to head out and give you guys some down time."

She nodded and watched him leave. She sagged against the fridge and closed her eyes.

"I miss you, too," she whispered.

Chapter Seventeen

They got Gideon to sleep after Lance and Avalon left. Serenity caught Lexi before she could escape to the quiet sanctuary of her room.

"Rough day?"

"The kind that makes me wish I wanted to take up drinking." Lexi groaned.

"Lance is a good guy."

"I know." If he weren't so good, it would be easier to move forward and forget what might have been.

"Why are you hesitating?" Serenity's voice sounded incredulous. She cast a quick glance at the living room and sat down in one of the kitchen chairs. Lowering her voice, she said, "You guys seem perfect for each other. He obviously adores you. He couldn't keep his eyes off you all night. And do I have to say it again? He's one of the good ones."

Serenity was the last person Lexi thought she would talk about this with. But maybe that was a good thing. Maybe it would help open up their relationship. God knew she needed to talk it out with someone.

"I feel blessed. That they caught the cancer early. That I'm able to do treatments and that the hysterectomy hopefully means I don't have to deal with this again. I feel blessed to have so many people who care about me." Lexi paused. "But I can't help but feel a little broken." She glanced toward the living room where Gideon was sleeping. "I wanted kids someday." Her eyes filled with tears and they were flowing down her cheeks before she knew what was happening. "I don't feel whole enough for Lance — or any man right now. I'm trying to let him go, though he isn't making it easy."

Lexi let herself cry into Serenity's shoulder. The weight of the last few days — Lance, the fire, the baby at the hospital, her chemo treatments — it all fell away in hot tears she couldn't seem to keep back.

Serenity rubbed her back, whispering, "It'll be okay, Lexi. You're tough. Everyone needs to fall apart sometimes and there's nothing wrong with that."

As the tears subsided, she took the napkin Serenity handed her and blew her nose. Wiping her eyes with a fresh tissue, she released a lungful of air. "Thanks. Sorry about that."

"Don't apologize. You've always got it all together. You always have. It was the one thing I most admired about you — and that drove me crazy."

Lexi blinked at her. "I don't have it together. Not even close."

"Then you fake it well. Lexi, when we were kids, you knew you wanted to be a nurse. You have always been comfortable in your own skin. I've wished I were more like you for a long time."

"I always thought you felt the opposite. There were many times I wondered if you hated me." She half expected her little sister to chuckle and tell her she was joking.

"Because I was the screw-up teenager who got pregnant and couldn't keep her boyfriend. I didn't go to college. I'm the single mom who will probably remain single for the rest of my life." She paused and shrugged. "The last thing I wanted was your advice because I knew you would be right and I still wouldn't be able to fix my life. I never hated you. I think, at times, I hated myself."

"Oh, Serenity. I never knew you felt that way." She tipped her head back and closed her eyes, her temple throbbing. "All those times I tried to help when you were pregnant. Trying to convince you he would come back was a mistake."

"I believed you, Lexi. I felt in my heart you were right. When you weren't... I decided I had a real reason to be angry at you." Serenity was crying now, sniffing and taking ragged breaths. "I was wrong to punish you for something that wasn't your fault. I'm sorry."

"Oh, sweetie, I am, too." Lexi gave her sister a hug — the kind of embrace that was long overdue. She cupped Serenity's face with her hands. "I love you. And I've missed my sister."

Serenity grinned through her tears. "I've missed you, too."

"No more letting stupid stuff get between us. Angry or not, we need to talk. Deal?"

"Deal." They shook hands and then hugged again.

Serenity blew her nose and took a deep breath. "I ran into him a couple of years ago."

"Gideon's father?"

"I hardly recognized him. He'd put on weight and shaved all that facial hair. But I knew it was him. We talked for a few minutes. He had no interest in Gideon at all. And you know what? I was okay with that. Because we're better off without him. Gideon is better off without a man who can't be the type of dad he deserves."

Lexi observed the baby sister that now seemed grown up. "I'm proud of you. You're an amazing mom. Gideon couldn't ask for better. I'm thankful you're my sister."

"Right back at you." Serenity laughed as they grabbed fresh napkins. "Look at us. We're a couple of real messes."

They sure were. But Lexi didn't care. She had her sister back.

~

Lance and Avalon headed back to his place after they had dinner at Lexi's. He'd had fun reconnecting with Avalon, but she still hadn't gone into many details about what had happened to her in Arizona.

It was driving him a little more than crazy. He studied her out of the corner of his eye. "When are you going to tell me more about this husband of yours?"

"Do you promise to listen and not judge?"

"To the absolute best of my abilities." He couldn't see her expression in the dark. "Then, if there's anything I can do to help, we can talk about that."

One thing had always been true of Avalon — you didn't push her into something she didn't want to do.

He tried to picture this Duke in Arizona and it was like staring into a black hole. A surge of protection went through him at the thought of anyone hurting his sister.

He didn't think she would say anything until her soft voice spoke above the noise of the road.

"Duke and his family own a farm right outside of Yuma, Arizona. They raise winter lettuce and broccoli mostly."

"You left Texas to marry a farmer. You see the irony in that, right?"

She slapped his arm. "Yes, I do. Do you want to hear this or not?"

It was all Lance could do to keep in a chuckle. He cleared his throat. "How did you end up down there in the first place?"

"After I left college, I bounced around between several jobs. I was driving through Yuma when I saw a job posting for one of the local farms. They needed help over the summer. They held classes for kids to teach them more about the agriculture in the area and its importance to our country. It sounded fun and different. I was sick of working fast food or indoor retail. It turned out that Duke's family was one of the main sponsors and he taught a few of them himself." She paused. "It was love at first sight. We got married July 15th."

Avalon working with kids. He could see that even if he couldn't picture her as a farmer's wife. "What happened?"

"I still believe we're in love. But we don't know each other. Not really. His family hates me." Her voice caught. "His mom told me I didn't belong there and I should leave before I ruined Duke's life."

Lance threw another glance at her. What kind of woman told her new daughter-in-law something that hateful?

"She sounds like a real winner."

"Right?"

"What are you going to do?"

"I don't want to quit. And honestly, I'm tempted to stay if only to spite her." Avalon moaned. "But I feel like it's me against the world over there. Duke is great, but he's having to deal with a lot concerning his family, too. My presence there is causing problems for him and I don't want to make his life more difficult."

"If you choose to leave him and move back here, are you doing it for you? Or for Duke? Or for his family?"

She considered him for a moment before saying, "That's a good point. I'm not even sure right now."

"Then that's an area you need to pray about. When you're faced with a confrontation, you tend to back down to avoid it. Don't let his mother determine what happens between you and Duke. A marriage is a big commitment. A divorce is no small thing, either."

Avalon leaned over to hug his arm and lay her head against his shoulder. "Thank you."

"For what?"

"For not judging me and for trying to help me see things in a different way. That's what I needed."

"Does Duke know you're here?"

"No. I said I needed time to think and didn't tell him where I was going."

"If you had, would he come after you?"

She thought about that. "Probably."

"That may be a key to the answer there, too. It sounds like he cares about you."

Avalon looked wistful.

"And you love him."

"I do."

"Things worth having are always worth fighting for."

~

Lance's thoughts were on Lexi. Using his lathe, he'd been working to transform the charred Chandler table legs into something for each member of the family. He'd made a lot of progress and hoped to finish the last two soon.

The workshop door opened and he watched as Tuck strode in.

"I've been seeing a lot of you lately. What's up?"

Tuck checked his watch. "I've got a couple of minutes and wanted to check in. Any progress with Lexi?"

Lance filled him in on the basics from the last few days. "I don't think ambushing her at her apartment for a third time is the right thing to do. We haven't even had the opportunity for a real conversation without being interrupted."

"The company you contracted is going into the house today to gut the kitchen and replace the flooring and walls. Everyone is moving back in on Saturday morning. We're having a family dinner that night since Lexi has to work Sunday evening." Tuck paused. "Consider yourself invited. Come by and I'll make sure you have a chance to talk to her."

Lance nodded. "I'll be there. Thanks, Tuck."

"Anytime."

~

Lexi got off work at six on Saturday morning. She went home, ate breakfast, and had no trouble going to sleep.

Her alarm went off in the afternoon, giving her plenty of time to take a shower, change into a pair of jeans and a dark blue shirt, and drive to the Chandler house.

Patty showed her the kitchen. A lot of progress had been made in the last few days. Damaged appliances had been removed and a new fridge plugged into a working outlet. Lexi smiled when she spotted the photo magnet in its new location.

Patty put an arm around her shoulders and gave her a squeeze. "Tuck said the contractors will work hard to get this finished before Thanksgiving. Praise God Lance had some connections or who knows what we would have done."

Lance. Just his name made her pulse quicken and her chest ache. He was a true friend no matter what happened between them. Just like he'd said he would be. Patty was still talking and Lexi did her best to focus on her words.

"I'm thinking about ordering a double oven this time around."

Lexi nodded with a smile. "That's a good plan." She glanced behind them to make sure Grams was out of earshot. "Is she doing okay about the table?"

"She's sad about it. But she's tough. She's gone through a lot worse and she's not letting it get her down." She paused. "We can all learn a lot from Grams and the way she's always handled challenges and loss in her life."

It was true. "With dignity, prayer, and by never giving up."

"Yep."

They heard the front door open and Lance's voice floated into the kitchen as he greeted people.

Lexi's shoulders sagged and Patty gave her a tighter squeeze.

"Grams isn't the only one who never gives up."

Patty chuckled. "You might have found a person who's as stubborn as you are." With a wink, she turned and joined the others in the living room.

Someone else approached Lexi. There was no mistaking the towering figure of Tuck. "I hate you."

He laughed loudly, resting an elbow on her shoulder. "No you don't."

"Don't be so sure."

"Come on, big sister. Hiding in here won't do you much good."

She tried to give him a stern look, but the grin on his face was too much and she ended up smiling at him in return. She gave him a nudge with her shoulder before walking into the living room.

Lance met her gaze with a warm smile, his eyes questioning her. She returned it with a small wave before averting her attention to Grams.

Tuck and Laurie had picked up the meal on the way there: barbecue summer sausage and brisket with baked beans and rolls. He told them all he figured they would eat enough sandwiches over the next month. They could put leftovers in the fridge and he would come by the next day with a microwave so they could at least heat food back up again.

Conversation centered on the work that would be done in the kitchen.

Rogue, was lying on the floor near Lexi, his eyes going from plate to plate in hopes of a scrap of food.

Lexi nudged him with her foot and gave him a wink. "I've got you covered, boy." She moved a bite of sausage to one side of her plate so she could save it for him.

Dessert was peach cobbler and vanilla ice cream.

At dinner, Gideon had only eaten rolls and cheese, but he put away a bowl of ice cream without complaint. Serenity chuckled at him and swiped a drip off his chin with her napkin.

Laurie approached Lexi and sat next to her on the couch. "When's your next session?"

Lexi thought a moment. "This coming Friday." She made a face. "At least it's the last one. I'm ready to be done."

"I imagine." Laurie was silent for a time. "I'm not going to get in the middle of things. But I wanted you to know that I'm happy to drive you to your session that day. Say the word."

Lexi regarded her sister-in-law. She had to be one of the sweetest, kindest women she'd ever known. Tuck had known what he was doing when he asked her to be his wife. The two of them seemed happy together. "I appreciate that, Laurie. Thank you. I'll take you up on it."

The ladies visited for a while about photography and a particularly difficult session Laurie had the week before.

"I have a new rule. No pot-bellied pigs allowed in my studio."

The story had Lexi laughing hard, tears flowing. "I wish I'd been there."

"Oh I wish you had, too. I'll send you a few of the

pictures when I get them processed. They aren't going on the website. I'm serious – no more farm animals."

Lexi was laughing. The image of a pot-bellied pig wearing a sunhat and running through Laurie's studio was one she wouldn't forget soon.

Lance had gone outside for something, taking Tuck with him. When they returned, each of them were carrying cardboard boxes. Lance scanned the room, his gaze settling on Grams.

They set the boxes down and Lance cleared his throat.

"I took the table back to my workshop like I promised I would. I hoped I could somehow repair it for you. I'm sorry to say that the fire damaged too much of the surface for me to salvage the table itself."

Grams was trying to hide her disappointment, but her chin quivered.

"There was enough wood spared for me to take it and transform the table into something for each of you. I hope you like them."

Lance carried his box over to Grams. "I used what I could of the top to make this for you. I know it's not the same, but I hope it helps relieve your loss."

They watched as he pulled out a wooden box that was two feet by two feet square. Lance had stained the wood so it was almost identical to the original. Grams reached for it and placed it gingerly on her lap. She ran her hand over the top of the box, lifting the hinged lid. When she looked inside, she gasped, tears springing to her eyes.

Patty stood. "What is it, Mom?" She put an arm around Grams' shoulders and peered into the box. "Lance, this is perfect."

Wiping tears from her eyes, Grams turned the box

and tilted it so others around the room could see it.

When Nicholas had made the table, he'd signed the bottom of it. Lance had taken that part of the table and used it to create the lid. Grams would be able to see his name every time she opened the box.

Grams ran a weathered finger over the signature while holding her locket in the other. She handed the box to Patty and stood. "This, young man, couldn't be more perfect." She hugged him tightly and pressed a kiss to his cheek. "Thank you for giving my Nicholas' table back to me."

"You're welcome, Grams."

There was no mistaking the moisture in Lance's eyes as he cleared his throat. "I have something for the rest of you, too." He passed out round trinket boxes he'd made to Tuck, Serenity, Patty, Lexi, and Gideon. "I used the table legs for these."

Lexi's hand brushed Lance's as she took the gift from him. It was perfect, every part sanded smooth and stained. She grasped the lid and lifted it, her eyes widening when she saw what was inside.

Nestled in a piece of cloth, she found the glass ball she'd seen at the renaissance festival. Tears stung the back of her eyelids as she touched the smooth glass.

Chapter Eighteen

L exi examined the object in her hands with awe. The trinket box alone was an amazing gift. But when she saw the glass ball, her heart skipped a beat. Not only had Lance noticed how much she'd liked it, but he had thought to buy it for her before they'd left the renaissance festival. His attention to details made Lexi feel treasured in a way she hadn't thought possible.

Her gaze rose to meet Lance's. His blue eyes were filled with emotion. Sadness, hope, and something else she couldn't quite identify swirled together. He studied her face with an intensity that made Lexi wonder what was going through his mind while simultaneously fearing what she might discover.

Serenity stood and gave him a hug followed by Tuck. "This is amazing, thank you."

"It's beautiful." Laurie said, looking at Grams' box. She turned her attention to Lance. "You outdid yourself. These are all special."

Lance rubbed a hand across his goatee. "I'm glad

everyone likes them."

Lexi could see his ears were flushed and knew he was embarrassed by all the attention. She was trying to decide what to say to him when her phone rang. Relief mixed with annoyance ran through her as she took it to the kitchen.

When the call was over, she went back into the living room. "Guys, I'm so sorry. I just got called into work. They have had two nurses call in sick and need someone to fill in for a few hours." She circled through the room, giving hugs to her family members. "Thank you guys for a fun evening. I'm glad things are beginning to return to normal here at the house."

Patty hugged Lexi close. "I wish you didn't have to leave so quickly."

"I know, Mom. Me, too. Don't count on me at church tomorrow. I have no idea how late I'll be working. I'll text you, though."

Patty nodded.

Lexi picked up her box and turned to Lance. Her heart thudded painfully in her chest as she approached him. She held the box he'd made her out in front as if it could act like a shield between them. "Thank you so much." She swallowed past the emotion building in her throat. "It's perfect." Lexi wanted to run, but knew that he deserved a hug for all of his hard work. Everyone else had given him one and it would be more awkward not to. She reached for him with one arm and turned her head, doing her best to keep it as brief as possible.

The moment his arms closed around her, every muscle in her body wanted to sink into him. She breathed in his scent — a combination of cedar and soap.

The embrace only lasted a moment, but before releasing her, Lance paused, his mouth close enough that she could feel the warmth of his breath on her ear. "I love you, Lex."

His words brought the sting of tears and stole the breath from her lungs. She stepped away from him, gave a final wave over her shoulder, and all but fled from the house before anyone tried to stop her.

When she got to the safety of her car, she took a tentative breath as hot tears trickled down her cheeks.

~

Lexi was only supposed to work a few hours at the hospital, but they didn't get a replacement in until nearly one in the morning. She was tired, but it was her heart that felt bruised.

Lance loved her. She'd known that for a while now, but hearing him say it was a completely different thing. It hurt because she knew that she was in love with him, too. But staying away was something she had to do — for him.

Lexi should have gone home, but she found herself going upstairs to the NICU. She knew that the newborn she'd helped stabilize was still receiving care. He'd been on her mind a lot and she thought going to see him would be good for both of them.

She spotted him quickly and was relieved to see that he was no longer intubated and appeared to be breathing on his own. Extra oxygen was being administered through a nasal cannula, taped firmly in place. The baby was sleeping, his face peaceful.

"You're from the ER?"

Lexi turned to find another nurse standing behind her. She nodded. "I was one of many who worked to stabilize this little guy. I wanted to see how he was doing."

"He's made significant improvements." The nurse went through and gave Lexi a general report on his condition. "They did find the parents who abandoned him. They are eager to relinquish their rights. We're hoping the little guy will be released in another day or two to a couple who'll foster him."

"Wow! So they already found someone?"

"That's what I've heard. Apparently a local couple who have been waiting to foster and eventually adopt a baby." The nurse smiled down at the boy fondly. "It looks like he's going to get his happily ever after."

Praise God! Lexi studied the baby's tiny features.

"Would you like to hold him? We usually have a couple of volunteers who come in to hold the NICU babies. We've found it makes a difference in their recovery time. We don't have any volunteers on the schedule for today."

Lexi looked from the nurse to the baby and back again. She surprised herself when she said, "I would love to hold him for a while."

The nurse smiled brightly. Lexi took a seat in a rocking chair nearby as the nurse lifted the baby and placed him in her arms, taking care to arrange the different tubes and monitor wires. "I'll be back to check on you in about fifteen minutes."

Lexi gave a nod without looking away from the tiny face. The baby boy opened his eyes briefly and yawned. He wiggled around in her arms and eventually settled. As he fell asleep again, his tiny mouth made suckling motions.

The warm weight of his body in her arms caused Lexi to relax in the chair. She found herself rocking it gently while humming. She stroked his tiny hand with a single finger.

Her foot stilled and the chair stopped as a realization came to Lexi. The baby's biological parents clearly could have children of their own, yet weren't able to care for or love the baby they had created. On the other hand, there was a couple who, for some reason or another, was unable to have children. Yet they hadn't given up hope that they would add to their family in a different way.

God took that couple's situation and brought them in touch with a life that desperately needed them.

The baby stirred in Lexi's arms and she started rocking him again.

"You'll never remember how you came into this world, little one." Lexi touched her cheek to the small tuft of hair on his head. "Hopefully all you'll know is the love of a dad and mom who waited a long time for you to come into their lives. You're going to be their miracle."

Lexi smiled and for the first time in months, she felt as though a weight had been lifted off her shoulders. Her heart felt light and goosebumps appeared on the surface of her arms.

Maybe God was using her situation to mold her into the person she needed to be. Maybe He was preparing her life so she could be part of a miracle like this someday.

As she continued to rock the baby, she prayed. "God, I haven't been very good at listening to you lately. If there's one thing I've learned, it's that I don't have control over a lot of things in my life. Yet You have managed to pull me through all of these challenges despite my stubborn pride. Help me to relinquish more control to You."

Without warning, a verse popped into her head. "Therefore do not worry about tomorrow, for tomorrow will worry about its own things." Matthew 6:34 — she remembered the pastor talking about it several months ago. At the time, it hadn't meant anything specific to her. Now, it resonated through every cell in her body.

That was exactly what she'd been doing — worrying about what might be. All of the doubts that had been playing through her head came back to her in a wave.

What if Lance decided having biological children was important? What if he changed his mind about her?

Lexi couldn't know what her future held. There was only one thing that worrying about it did for her — it robbed her of what was right in front of her in the here and now.

Lance.

Maybe it was time to place her hopes in God and let Him take care of her future for a change.

~

Tuck caught Lance before he'd had a chance to climb into his Jeep after church Sunday morning.

"Have you heard from Lexi?"

Lance had watched Lexi walk out the door at the Chandler house the night before. The call Lexi received couldn't have come at a worse time. He'd hoped she would see his gift and then he could talk to her. Knowing his opportunity was quickly slipping through his fingers, he'd whispered that he loved her. He wasn't sure what he'd hoped would happen once the words were out of his mouth. But Lexi had left quickly leaving him with nothing to cling to but his doubts.

"Not a word."

"Sorry, man. I really thought you two would get a chance to talk last night." Tuck paused. "I'll go by her place and find out what's going on."

"Don't. The ball's in her court, now."

Tuck stepped around to stand in front of his best friend. "You're giving up on her?"

"No. But I can't convince her to do or feel a certain way. And neither can you. It has to be her decision."

It pained Lance to say it, but it was the truth. He'd done everything he could to show and tell her how he felt.

"She'll come around, Lance. I've always felt you two were meant to be together."

He hoped Tuck was right. If she didn't, he prayed he would know how to survive when she walked away with his heart.

Lance spent the majority of the afternoon at home. He alternated between praying for his relationship with Lexi and trying to push her from his mind. When he blinked at the page of a book he'd been trying to read for the last thirty minutes, he tossed it down on the coffee table.

He thought about the projects waiting for him at the workshop. Maybe if he worked and got something accomplished, it would help. It was just after four when he took off in his Jeep.

As he pulled to a stop in front of the building, his eyes were drawn to the door.

Lexi was sitting on the steps, her arms around her knees, drawing them to her chest. Her chin rested on her arm as a blue floral handkerchief fluttered in the breeze at the nape of her neck.

Lance's chest felt tight as he stepped to the ground and he walked towards her. "How long have you been here?"

She tilted her left wrist to look at her watch. "Since two or so."

"Lex, that was over two hours ago. Why didn't you text me?"

She shrugged and made no motion to stand. Lance unlocked the door and retrieved a bottle of water from the small fridge he kept in the office. He handed it to her and offered a hand to help her up. Lexi accepted, rising to her feet.

"Thank you," she said. She twisted the lid off and took a long drink. After replacing the lid, her eyes flitted to his and away again. "Can we talk?" She clutched the bottle of water in both hands, rotating it between them. "Please?"

Lance had an empty feeling in the pit of his stomach as he stood to the side and motioned her inside the workshop. When he reached for a chair, she shook her head emphatically.

"I would rather stand."

"Okay." He said the word slowly. He resisted the need to reach out and touch her arm. Lance studied her profile. He admired the dark eyelashes that delicately framed her lovely eyes. He wished she would look at him.

Lexi took a deep breath. "Communication has not

been my strong point lately. You're my best friend. Instead of shutting down, I should have talked to you about it. I'm sorry."

That was what he'd missed the most. Being able to talk to Lexi and share their thoughts. He nodded once. "Apology accepted." She raised her chin to look at him. "What happened at the renaissance festival? I thought we had something really great between us. Something that day scared you. Or made you change your mind. What was it?"

She took a deep breath. "You're the last of the Davenport men. I didn't know that until I spoke with your sisters at the festival. I've watched you with Gideon. You'll make a great dad, Lance. Someday you'll want kids you can take fishing or teach them how to make things like your dad taught you." Her gaze collided with his. "That was the day I truly realized that I couldn't give you any of that."

The familiar ache assaulted his heart as he listened to her words. "Not having a biological child isn't the end of the world." Losing her, now that was a different story.

"I was scared."

He could tell it took a lot out of her to admit that. She'd faced her fears for as long as he'd known her. A lot of reasons for her silence had filled his imagination, but fear on her behalf wasn't one of them. "What were you scared of?"

Lexi clung to the water bottle as if it were a lifeline. Her eyes were on it as she wrestled with her words.

"I was scared that, five years from now, you might change your mind about us. About me."

Chapter Nineteen

Lance surprised Lexi when he took the water bottle from her hands and put it down on a chair nearby. He placed a firm hand on each of her shoulders and waited until she'd raised her eyes to his face. There were a lot of reactions she'd expected from him. But the gentle smile and the determination emanating from his blue eyes surprised her.

"Girl, I've been in love with you for more than a decade. If there's one thing you can say about me, I have staying power. Or I'm obsessive. Pick whichever works more in my favor." He gave her a wink.

Lexi chuckled and fiddled with the edge of her handkerchief absently.

He slid both of his hands down her arms to take her hands in his. "What changed? Why did you decide to come and talk to me?"

"Do you remember the abandoned baby I told you about?" He nodded. "He's still at the hospital. I went to see him today and ended up holding him for almost an hour. He's going to live with a couple who have been wanting a child for a long time. I realized that, even though what happened to that baby was horrible, God is using it to bring about a miracle for three different lives." Lexi paused, searching for the right words. "I was worried about my cancer. I was convinced you would come to your senses some day and change your mind about me. I had focused so much on the future that I was missing out on the present. I guess I realized that I should probably leave that to God. I'm obviously not qualified for the job."

Lance reached to gently tweak her earlobe and ran the back of his fingers down her jaw. "What does that mean, Lex?"

His touch made her pulse race as determination flooded every fiber of her being. "I love you, too. With all of my heart."

A brilliant smile lit up his face and he hooked an arm around her waist to draw her close. "Come here, you."

When their lips met, he poured every ounce of love he had into the caress. She melted into him as he deepened their kiss. He tugged the handkerchief free and let it fall as he cradled the back of her head with his free hand.

He placed kisses on the corner of her mouth and behind her ear. "Does this mean you're going to fire Laurie so I can take you to your last chemo session?"

Lexi moved her head back, doing her best to maintain a serious expression. "You've been there for all the games, you may as well finish the season."

Lance laughed then, holding her close and kissing her until his good sense told him to quit.

~

"She married a farmer in Arizona? Wow." Lexi was lounging on her bed, a bag of chips nearby, and her cell phone to her ear. It was early Monday morning. She'd been off work only thirty minutes and had called Lance as soon as she got home. They had a lot of catching up to do. "What did your parents have to say?"

"At first, Avalon swore me to secrecy. But I convinced her to talk to our parents. They took it well, though Mom's disappointed she couldn't be there for the wedding. I think it went as well as it possibly could have given the circumstances. Avalon woke up yesterday morning and left for a couple of hours. When she got back, she was determined to return to Arizona. Hopefully everything will work out and we'll get to meet this husband of hers soon."

Lexi sat up and crossed her legs. "It's good she decided to go back."

"I think so, too. I said that, if she needed me, I could come down for a few days in December. She said she'd let me know."

"You're a good brother." She picked up the bag of chips and deposited it on the nightstand, moving out of arms reach before she ate them all. "Speaking of little sisters and hearing about their lives…" She told him about her conversation with Serenity the other night and about how she felt growing up.

"It sounds like things are going well between the two of you now."

"They are." Lexi smiled. It'd been a long time since she could think of Serenity and not feel anxious or sad. "I can't wait for Sunday. It means I'll be done with chemotherapy. And Gideon's birthday party is after church."

"I'm glad I was invited."

"You're practically part of the family." The moment the words were out, Lexi felt her face grow warm. "You know what I mean."

His deep chuckle reached her ears and she could imagine his blue eyes sparkling. "Yes, I do."

Lexi yawned, unable to suppress it. "Sorry about that."

"No worries. It's been a long, eventful week."

"It has." She paused. She'd been checking into different employment options the last few days. To her surprise, she'd found several opportunities. "I'm thinking about finding another job."

"Really? What brought that on?"

"A lot of things." She laid back against her pillow and stretched her legs out. "There's more to life than working. I love what I do and I love helping kids. But the rest of my life fits in around work instead of the other way around. I never have a predictable schedule with the hospital. And these twelve-hour days are killing me."

"All valid points." She could hear him take a drink of something. "What do you have in mind?"

"There are several openings around town. One I'm looking into is at the main pediatric clinic. They are a great group of people and Serenity always speaks highly of them. There are three pediatricians in the practice there and I would float around to whoever needs me."

"I'll bet the hours are better, too."

She laughed. "Oh, yes. They open at eight. I would have to be there at seven-thirty, with an hour for lunch, and they close at five. I could get used to that. Monday through Friday, though they have clinic hours Saturdays noon to five. But I guess everyone rotates and I would only work one Saturday per month."

"It sounds about perfect. What about the pay?"

"It's a pay cut, but I'll be gaining a lot of hours in my life. I think it'll be worth it."

"So do I. If it gives you more time to spend with the local carpenter, you won't hear any complaints from me."

Lexi chuckled. "I already submitted my resume. I'm hoping I'll hear from them this week."

"They'd be crazy to not hire you."

"I appreciate that."

They were both silent for a few moments until Lance's voice came over the line. "I should let you go. You need to get some sleep before your shift tonight. Keep me updated on the job front, huh?"

"I will. Thanks again for the beautiful box and the glass ball. They're perfect."

"You're welcome. I love you, Lex."

"I love you, too."

~

Lexi had been asleep an hour when her cell phone rang after nine that morning. She didn't recognize the number. Sitting up in bed, she cleared her throat and answered it.

The last thing she expected was for the pediatrician's office to be calling asking her to come by that day for an interview. They scheduled it for one in the afternoon.

She desperately needed more sleep, but had to get up long enough to make a list of things to do before the interview. Her mind ran through a list of questions they might ask her. At least, when it came to pediatrics, she was confident of her knowledge and abilities.

If she said she wasn't nervous, however, she'd be lying. She'd been working at the hospital since she'd left nursing school. A change was exactly what she needed, but it was also a little scary.

She sent a text to Lance.

"I have an interview at one. Please pray that, if this is what God wants me to do, all goes well."

Five minutes later, she got a text back.

"I'll be praying. You'll do great! Text me after when you can, okay?"

"I will. Thanks! I'm going to go and try to get some sleep."

~

"They offered me the job!" Lexi's excited voice came through Lance's phone. "I'm supposed to go in tomorrow to sign papers and should start work two weeks from today."

"That's great, Lex! I'm proud of you." He inspected the calendar and circled the day, adding a note. "You're almost done with chemo and then, a week later, you'll have a new job. God's giving you a fresh start."

"You're right. Sometimes, going forward, everything looks like a mess. But then we get through it, look back, and realize He knew exactly what He was doing."

"Which is a good thing because if we were left to our own devices, we'd mess it all up."

She laughed. "I have no doubt that you're right. I hate to run, but I need to get in for my shift. Dinner tomorrow?"

"Absolutely. But I want to take you somewhere nice. You know, a restaurant that doesn't resemble a hospital cafeteria."

"What? Are you getting tired of dry enchiladas and slightly soggy tacos?"

"Maybe. But the company always makes it worth it."

Lexi giggled. "I'll text you."

They ended the call and Lance knew he was grinning like a fool. His girl was getting a new job, she was almost done with her treatments, and he would see her for dinner tomorrow. Yes, life was good.

~

"Are you ready for this?" Lance reached for Lexi's hand as they rode the elevator and walked down the hall at the cancer center.

"Very." It was her last chemotherapy session and she looked forward to having the treatments behind her. She placed her free hand on her head. "I wonder how long it'll take before my hair grows back again."

"We'll just have to wait and see. I've gotten used to it now." Lance rubbed the top of her head. "Maybe you should keep it shaved."

She raised an eyebrow at him. "Only if you do the same thing. And I'm talking your head and your goatee."

He covered his face with his hands. "The head, maybe. The goatee? Never."

They stopped walking and Lexi gave him a peck

on his scruffy chin. "I'm glad. I like it."

Lance kissed her before taking her hand again.

The nurse got her set up with the IV and took more blood samples. "Did Doctor Ravenhill talk to you about the CA 125 test and CT scan?"

"She mentioned the test. It's a tumor marker."

"That's right." The nurse wrote Lexi's name on the tube of blood. "She's going to send it off and the numbers will give us an idea of how well the chemotherapy has worked. It's especially helpful in cases of ovarian cancer."

Lexi nodded. She'd read about the test and knew that, while it wasn't always accurate, higher than normal levels in the bloodstream would at least give her doctor a red flag and warrant further investigation.

The nurse continued, "You'll come back for the test every three months for a year, then every year for as long as the doctor feels that it's necessary."

Lance squeezed Lexi's hand. "What about the CT scan?"

"Doctor Ravenhill always orders a CT scan after the last session of chemotherapy. She will check it to make sure everything looks normal and will use it as a base of comparison if any future scans are necessary."

Lexi vaguely remembered the doctor mentioning the scan. She hadn't realized it would be today.

She watched the nurse leave and looked at Lance. "I think those tests will be nerve wracking for a while. I wonder if I'll ever get to a point where I won't worry about the cancer coming back."

Lance motioned for Lexi to scoot over and lounged beside her. She laid her head against his chest and listened to the comforting sound of his heartbeat.

He rubbed her shoulder and kissed her temple. "I don't know. But you have to live your life and trust that everything is going to be fine. God brought us this far. We're in it together."

Lexi tipped her head up to look at Lance. "You know, this is the first session I haven't counted down the minutes."

"Oh yeah?" He shifted so he could kiss her. "I wish I could have held you like this every time."

They talked about Gideon's birthday party and the wood burning that Peter was learning. Lexi dozed off in Lance's arms for a short while.

When the nurse removed the IV from her arm, Lexi flexed it. "That's it." She stood and turned to find Lance grinning at her

"That's it." He picked her up and spun her in a circle. He brushed a wayward tear from her cheek with the pad of his thumb. "You made it."

Chapter Twenty

Tuck snatched a chocolate chip cookie off the plate on the counter and ate it in a single bite. "When do you hear about the test results?"

"Hopefully early next week." Lexi would try and not focus on hearing from the doctor's office until after Wednesday. She was kidding herself. There was no doubt she would be waiting on the edge of her seat for the call beginning Monday morning. She knew everything would come back okay, but getting that confirmation felt like the last step in putting things behind her.

Gideon ran by with a fistful of colorful balloons. He released them in the living room, watched as each of them bounced to a stop on the ceiling, then jumped to gather them again.

Laurie snapped a few pictures. "I love how he's so joyful in everything he does."

They laughed as the boy ran down the hallway to his room, balloons floating behind him.

Serenity smiled proudly. "He's been looking forward to his birthday party for a while. We had it circled on the calendar and he's tapped on that day for the last two weeks." She checked to see he was still in his room. "I'll get the gifts out quick. Tuck, will you give me a minute and then let the birthday boy know he can open his presents?"

"You bet!"

When they were ready, Tuck went to find his nephew. Rumbling preceded him when Gideon came running into the room. He slid on his knees in front of the brightly-wrapped packages.

Lexi took a seat on the floor, close enough to watch the unwrapping, but far enough away to give Serenity, Patty, and Grams the front row seats.

"Do you mind if I join you?"

Lance smiled down at her and she patted the carpet next to her.

"Not at all."

He sat and leaned over to bump her shoulder with his.

They watched as Gideon opened the first two. The third one was the gift that Lexi had chosen for him. She'd put it in a large cardboard box that was nearly as tall as he was. She laughed as he struggled to open it. When he rescued the set of train bedding from the box, a grin appeared on his face.

Serenity gave her an approving nod.

Lexi got a kick out of Gideon insisting on dragging the bedding to his room before coming back to open another gift. "You know what I like about Gideon that you don't see in a lot of kids?"

Lance bumped her shoulder again with his and winked. "What's that?"

"I like how he opens a gift and doesn't immediately toss it aside for the next one. He wants to inspect it and see how it works."

They watched as he opened the rest of his presents, finishing with a train-themed mug and a large container of animal crackers from Lance. Gideon promptly opened the crackers and wasted no time in tasting one.

Serenity led Gideon around to tell each of them thank you for the gifts and prompted him to give hugs.

Afterwards, Gideon grabbed an armful of new toys and took them to his room. While he was gone, Serenity turned to address the room.

"Okay, we'll have cake here in a few minutes. Gideon's fine with songs this year. But no clapping or cheering at the end."

Everyone nodded their understanding.

Lexi remembered his birthday two years ago. They had all started to sing 'Happy Birthday' like they had before and the poor little guy had dissolved into sobs. It took over an hour to get him consoled. No one could figure out exactly what had brought that on, but each year was a little different and sometimes they couldn't anticipate everything. There was only one certainty when it came to autism: expect the unexpected.

Lance stood and reached a hand down to help Lexi up. As soon as she was on her feet, he managed a quick kiss before Serenity brought out the cake.

"That's so cute! He'll love it!" Laurie took a picture of the train cake, a number five candle on it.

Gideon approached it with a grin and got as close as he could. He touched the frosting at the base with a single finger.

"Okay, Gideon. We're going to sing you happy birthday. Then you can blow out the candle and eat cake. Are you ready?"

Gideon watched his mom expectantly as she started them all in the song. He watched them, his eyes going to each person in the room, as they sang. When they ended the song, he grinned and blew hard at the candle.

Lexi was sure saliva had been expelled with the air but knew no one would care. "Good job, big guy!" She looked over to find Serenity with tears in her eyes. She put an arm around her sister and gave her a hug.

"I can't believe my baby is five years old." Serenity sniffed. "He did well with everything, too. I'm proud of him."

"You should be! He's a great kid."

Serenity smiled through her tears. "Thank you."

"And I think you can call today's party a success."

"Yes, I think so." Serenity stood and watched her son devour his piece of cake, blue and red icing all over his chin.

She spoke loudly enough for everyone to hear. "Thank you all for coming!"

"Are you kidding?" Tuck swiped a finger in frosting and dabbed it onto Gideon's nose. "I wouldn't have missed it for the world."

The boy tried to stick his tongue as far as he could, hoping to lick the end of his nose. His antics had everyone giggling before Laurie took a napkin and wiped off his face.

Lexi followed Patty into the kitchen to clean up. When they were done, Patty motioned for Lexi to join her out on the back porch.

"I wanted to talk to you for a few minutes," she said, taking a seat in one of the patio chairs. Lexi followed suit. "I'm thankful you're done with chemotherapy."

"Me, too! It's been a long few months."

"You know, when you first told us about your surgery, all I could think of was your dad's fight with cancer. It was ugly." She paused. "I wouldn't wish what he went through on an enemy. Much less my own daughter." Her voice caught and she cleared her throat.

Lexi reached for her hand. "Mom, you don't have to talk about this."

Patty gave her a smile. "I had nightmares every night for a week. Reliving those last days with your dad. Not knowing what would happen to you."

"I know, Mom. Praise God, this time it was different."

"He's taken this whole thing and used it for a lot of good. Think about your relationship with Serenity. That's an answer to prayer right there."

"Yes, it is. Repairing our relationship is something I never thought would happen. It goes to show that, in everything, there's always hope."

"Let's not forget how it's brought you and Lance together, too."

Lexi wasn't going to argue with that. "There was one side effect from the chemotherapy I didn't mind so much."

"Oh? What's that?"

Lexi stretched her legs out and clasped her hands behind her head. "I haven't had to shave my legs in weeks." She shrugged.

Patty laughed until there were tears in her eyes.

~

Lance chased Gideon around one side of the chair while Tuck went the other way. They met at the back and surrounded the squealing little boy. Lance picked him up. "He's mine. Mine!"

"I don't think so." Tuck grabbed onto his feet and pulled.

"Well, if you want him, you'll have to catch him." Lance gave Tuck a wink.

Tuck backed off a step or two and Lance made a big deal of tossing Gideon into the air. It was only a few inches. But to a five-year-old, he was sailing through the air to land in his uncle's arms.

Tuck tickled him and then set him down. The men watched as he ran off.

Lance jerked a thumb in his direction. "I think all that cake has gone to his head." He scanned the house for Lexi and didn't see her anywhere. A quick tally and he realized Patty was missing, too.

"They went in the backyard," Grams said, winking at him.

"Thanks!"

When he got to the screen door, he saw both women laughing hard, nearly sliding out of their chairs. He opened the door a little. "Are you ladies okay out here?"

"Oh, yeah. Everything is going smoothly." Lexi snorted and both women started laughing again.

Patty stood and leaned down to give her daughter a hug. Wiping her eyes, she opened the screen door the rest of the way. "Come on out, Lance. I need to go get something to drink. You can keep Alexis company."

"Yes, ma'am."

He held the door open for her and then sat down in the now-vacated chair. "It's nice to see you this happy."

"It's been a good day." She leaned her head back against the chair and closed her eyes. The gentle wind moved the leaves in the tree above her, causing shadows to dance on her face.

Lance got up to stand in front of her and placed a hand on either arm of the chair. Those dark brown eyes of hers opened, focusing on him.

"Have I mentioned lately how beautiful you are?" And kissable. Incredibly kissable. He touched her chin with one finger.

"Are you sure the sun isn't blinding you right now?" She rubbed the top of her bald head with both hands, a teasing little grin on her face.

"Absolutely sure." His lips sought hers, caressing them gently. She placed a hand on the back of his neck to draw him closer.

The back door opened. Lance groaned before he broke their kiss and stood up. He found Tuck standing in the doorway, a knowing smirk on his face. "I didn't mean to interrupt."

"Yeah, I'll bet." Lance winked.

"I was wondering if you wanted in on a friendly little game of basketball."

Lance took in the pink flush of Lexi's cheeks and couldn't stop the smile on his face. "Only if you can talk Laurie into playing two-on-two. I'm not going anywhere without my girl here."

"I bet that can be arranged." Tuck grinned and

ducked back inside.

Lexi stood and put an arm around his waist. "Thanks for being there for me through all of this. I don't know what I would have done without you."

He bowed before taking her hand and kissing it. "It was an honor, my lady. There's nowhere else I want to be than by your side."

About the Author

Melanie D. Snitker has enjoyed writing fiction for as long as she can remember. She started out writing episodes of cartoon shows that she wanted to see as a child and her love of writing grew from there. She and her husband live in Texas with their two children who keep their lives full of adventure, and two dogs who add a dash of mischief to the family dynamics. In her spare time, Melanie enjoys photography, reading, crochet, baking, archery, camping and hanging out with family and friends.

http://www.melaniedsnitker.com
https://twitter.com/MelanieDSnitker
https://www.facebook.com/melaniedsnitker

Melanie's Other Books

Calming the Storm
(A Christian Romance Novel)

Finding Peace
(Love's Compass: Book One)

Made in the USA
San Bernardino, CA
15 October 2015